Praise for *DC Trip*

"*DC Trip* is smart, funny, sexy, and sweet. Sara Benincasa has written a hilarious, bighearted novel about an essential high school experience."

> —Tom Perrotta, author of *Election* and *Little Children*

"The perfect, frothy blend of teen angst, adult drama, and whip-smart social commentary. This novel is a trip in every sense."

> —Diablo Cody, Academy Award-winning writer of
> *Juno*, and author of *Candy Girl*

"I'm an expert on the subject of girls, being married to one, having dated several, and now the father of a tween. As an expert, I can tell you with absolute certainty that Sara Benincasa has being a young female down. She is hilarious and insightful and smart—all traits the ladies I love share, although *DC Trip* transcends gender. I read and loved it and I'm a BOY!!! (A very famous and attractive boy.)"

> —Michael Ian Black, comedian

"Sara Benincasa's *DC Trip* is as wicked, dirty, funny and surprisingly poignant as her comedy. It's a wild, hilarious, and very grown-up ride into the world of teenagers and the adults charged with their care. Read it and laugh your ass off."

> —Jill Soloway, creator of
> Golden Globe award-winning series *Transparent*

"*DC Trip* is the adult book about high school you never knew you needed." —*Playboy*

★"This is a light yet deep novel that looks at the intricacies of both high school cliques and adult relationships. A fantastic add to fiction collections, this would be a great YA crossover for older teens (profanity and sexual situations are dealt with very well)." —*School Library Journal*, starred review

"The hilarious Benincasa's second book will give you all the field trip feelings (which, let's face it, are some of the strongest feelings humans ever experience). The protagonist is a new teacher daunted by the wild high schoolers she's chaperoning in the nation's capital—among her charges are three sopho-mores full of the spunk and daring inspired by being away from home for the first time." —*Glamour*

"Benincasa . . . creates situations that are jarringly outlandish, but still believable enough to be hilarious. . . . A breezy, charming novel." —*BUST*

"At times ribald, mischievous, and gross, *DC Trip* is never cynical, and it even occasionally gently tweaks its own lefty identity politics. The book deserves to be counted among *Me and Earl and the Dying Girl*, *King Dork*, and *The Perks of Being a Wallflower* as . . . novels that have raised the . . . bar by not insulting their target audiences, while still feeling universally relevant enough to make a man in his late thirties laugh out loud while reading it on the New York City subway." —Reason.com

DC TRIP

SARA BENINCASA

ADAPTIVE BOOKS

AN IMPRINT OF ADAPTIVE STUDIOS • CULVER CITY, CA

Copyright © 2015 Adaptive Studios
This paperback edition published in 2016

Visit us on the web at www.adaptivestudios.com

Library of Congress Cataloging-in-Publication Data 2015943072

ISBN 978-1-945293-07-8
Ebook ISBN 978-1-9864484-5-4

Printed in the United States of America

Designed by Neuwirth & Associates

Adaptive Books
3578 Hayden Avenue, Suite 6
Culver City, CA 90232

10 9 8 7 6 5 4 3 2 1

For Gretchen Rae Bauer Stanford and Rachel Sivan Perry, who did nothing that resembles anything in this book, aside from being excellent friends then and now.

And for three great high school educators, who did nothing that resembles anything in this book, aside from being excellent role models: Ms. Jennifer Peck-Nolte; Dr. William Fernekes; and especially my grandfather, the late, great Joseph Donnelly.

FROM: Alicia Deats
TO: Karen Henry
SUBJECT: Buckle up, it's gonna be a wild ride

Hi Karen. You may be wondering why I'm sending this message to your private email instead of the school email, since it's about the sophomore class trip. I know we try to keep our faculty mentoring relationship separate from our friendship, which is good because I doubt the principal would appreciate us hanging out in the faculty lounge and talking about how I got you high the night after your first faculty meeting in August. Nor does the principal need to hear us gossip about Hot Brad the Yoga Teacher at our new favorite studio downtown.

By the way, did you know some people in Flemington still consider yoga to be a "cult-like" activity? Not the principal, obviously, but some of the parents. You'd think an upper-middle-class town in suburban New Jersey would be a little more educated about these things, but I seriously had kids' parents complain when I taught yoga workshops during gym class my first year here. (You may ask why the hell a social studies teacher would give up her free period in order to teach downward-facing dog to a bunch of hormonal beast children, but I wanted to be Little Miss Helpful.)

Those conservative parents still try to mess with my curriculum each year. And you should hear how they freak out about Patti Bump's health and human sexuality course. I don't know how I ended up in the only consistently Republican county in New Jersey, but life takes us on weird journeys.

Okay, so, we haven't really gotten to talk about the sophomore class trip in person. You've been running around trying to be the perfect first-year teacher in spite of my warning that this is a totally impossible task. You say yes to everything anyone asks of you, and I swear to Goddess by next year I'm going to have taught you how to say no, Karen. But I get why you'd want to co-chaperone the sophomore class trip. I did the same thing my first year. It sounded fun, it was a chance to get out of the classroom and travel, and the stipend they offer you is surprisingly hefty.

When I went on my first, and to date only, sophomore class trip, I was your age—twenty-three. I was idealistic and hopeful and excited, just like you. And I'm not going to say that the trip diminished my love for teaching or for this school. In fact, some amazing things happened that changed my life in fantastic ways and made me love this gig even more.

It was also a royal pain in the butt.

You know those girls who visit me each year, the ones I introduced you to at Christmas—Gertie, Sivan, and Rachel? They were my favorite students my first year. They're still my all-time favorite students, although Katy Henk in third period rivals them in greatness. Well, turns out my favorite students were also my most mischievous ones. I just didn't fully realize it at the time, because they hid some stuff pretty well. But a few years back we all got drunk the day after Thanksgiving and they spilled everything. *Everything.*

Then again, so did I.

You know how I get when I drink.

Anyway, in the interest of full disclosure, and of hopefully protecting you from the rude awakening I got, I'm going to tell you everything that happened on my first and only sophomore class trip. You are to share this tale with absolutely no one. I one hundred percent trust you, and not just because we have always spotted each other during handstand in yoga class.

I suggest reading this with a glass of wine. Not two or

three glasses—a hungover trip chaperone is an unhappy trip chaperone. But one glass. Sip it slowly and savor the magic I'm about to drop on you.

And in case anything crazy happens on your trip—don't say I didn't warn you.

Love you,
Alicia

DAY ONE

By the time Gertie, Sivan, and Rachel got to school, the rest of the sophomores were already there. The other students were gathered in a pack on the front lawn of the school, listening to Mr. Kenner and Ms. Deats, so Gertie, Sivan, and Rachel hurried to catch up with them.

"Ah, Gertrude Santanello-Smith, Sivan Finkelstein, Rachel Miller," Mr. Kenner said, ignoring the horrified look on Gertie's face when he used her real name. "How nice of you to join us."

"It's my fault we're late, Mr. Kenner," Rachel said sweetly, batting her eyelashes at him. "I'm really sorry. My mother was sick this morning and I had to make breakfast for my father before he left for the church elders committee meeting." Gertie marveled at how easily a lie formed on Rachel's lips—they actually were late only because Rachel had taken forever to fix her hair.

Sivan stared at the ground, because she wasn't good at maintaining eye contact with disapproving adults. She just wasn't used to it—adult disapproval was a real rarity in Sivan's experience. Her professor parents adored her so much they'd even started a PFLAG chapter in her honor at their synagogue, which made Sivan deeply uncomfortable.

Rachel wasn't particularly accustomed to adult disapproval, either, but she had no fear of it—not when she was sneaking out of class to blow football players in the bathroom; not when she was doing lines of coke off the actual altar in the chapel at church camp; and certainly not when she was fifteen minutes late for a fucking school trip. Rachel had the kind of blond hair and blue eyes and perfect skin and perfect tits that made her a standout in any crowd, and more than one good Christian son (and father) entertained impure thoughts as she stood in front of the huge megachurch congregation, singing a solo. Meanwhile, her parents beamed proudly from their seats, convinced their daughter was the most religious person since actual Jesus.

"Okay, Rachel," Mr. Kenner said, in a way that made it obvious he didn't believe her. "Well, you're all here, so let's get to the important stuff. All of you need to listen up and keep your eyes on me and Ms. Deats. That means you too, Sivan." Sivan looked up and nodded obediently. Of the three of them, Sivan was probably the one Mr. Kenner liked the most. As long as you tried hard in his class, he liked you, even if you weren't good at math. That's why he was most tolerant of Sivan, who tried very hard and happened to be great at math too. Gertie gave it a reasonable shot and made B's, so she was all right by Mr. Kenner most of the time. Gertie gave everything in life a reasonable shot and played by the rules without fail. But Rachel doodled pictures of cute animals on her tests and never showed up for the early-morning or after-school tutoring sessions Mr. Kenner offered. She also never did any extra credit assignments to bring up her grade. Therefore, he was obviously indisposed to any fondness toward her, though it seemed to bother her not one bit. Rachel found most men rather amusing, and Mr. Kenner was no exception.

Then there was Ms. Deats, who was just a real sweetheart. She was nice to everybody, even the kids who were rowdy or disrespectful or made fun of her hippie jewelry. Today she was in top twenty-three-year-old hippie form, wearing a long, flowing purple skirt, Birkenstock sandals, a T-shirt that read BE THE CHANGE, and big Native American dreamcatcher earrings that you just knew she'd bought on a reservation when she went for a sweat lodge ceremony or something where the locals charged the annoying tourists an exorbitant fee for an "authentic" native experience. She was the kind of person who had a story about every article of clothing she wore. She'd tell you too, if you so much as glanced at a chunky turquoise-and-silver bracelet or a rose quartz ring.

"Okay, students," Ms. Deats said, clasping her hands together and smiling brightly. "You all know the three strikes, you're out rule, but the principal requires us to go over it every single time we take you on a trip." She gave a little chuckle, as if to indicate that she thought it was silly.

"That's because it's very important," Mr. Kenner said seriously, furrowing his brow. "Three behavioral infractions, and you're suspended. School trips require good behavior because you are representing Flemington High School to the entire world, especially in Washington, D.C." He glanced sideways at Ms. Deats. "And there's an additional rule for this trip."

She winced a little. "Well, I'm sure it won't be a problem."

"We need to tell them anyway," Mr. Kenner said.

"Okay," Ms. Deats said reluctantly. "Well, the principal has decided that any student who gets three infractions will not only be suspended from school, but will take summer school classes before being permitted to enter the junior year. This will go on your permanent record."

The students looked at each other in disbelief. Some of them groaned. Others said, "What?"

"That's not fair!" Brooklynn said. She was standing with Peighton and Kaylee, and they were wearing matching blue T-shirts and white short shorts, because of course they were. What's the point of being the most popular, best-looking, shittiest girls in school if you don't wear identical outfits?

"I mean, I'm obviously not going to do anything wrong," Brooklynn said, laughing her nasty little laugh and casting a snide glance at Rachel. "But for some of the people who are . . . prone to misbehavior. It doesn't seem fair."

"It seems fair to me," Mr. Kenner said. "That's the rule."

"Well, I'm sure people will behave themselves," Brooklynn said sweetly, staring at Rachel again. "Even the ones who don't usually exercise self-control." Rachel looked right back at her and smiled, waving.

"Don't piss her off," Gertie hissed to Rachel.

"I don't care how she feels," Rachel said at a normal volume. "If she has actual feelings."

"What's that, Rachel?" Mr. Kenner asked sharply.

"I'm really looking forward to the Air and Space Museum!" Rachel chirped.

Mr. Kenner's expression softened a bit. He even had a hint of a smile. "It's my favorite museum in the world," he said, and you could tell he meant it. "The history of the National Aeronautics and Space Administration is fascinating."

"I agree," Rachel said. "So much beautiful math."

Sivan tried not to snort. Rachel was so ridiculous sometimes.

When Sivan looked up, Peighton was glowering at her. Brooklynn was staring daggers at Rachel. And Kaylee, who was the stupidest member of the cuntriad, was narrowing her eyes at Gertie. Kaylee had no reason to hate Gertie other than that Peighton already hated Sivan and Brooklynn already hated Rachel.

Sivan sighed. It was going to be a long trip.

After the usual directions about behavior and logistics, the students crammed into the bus, finding seats in the complex teen dance of social hierarchy. Alicia and Brian stood on either side of the aisle in the front. Once everybody was seated, Brian cleared his throat loudly. The kids all knew what that meant, and they quieted down and looked at him expectantly.

"I've chaperoned this sophomore D.C. trip for five years," he said. "And in that time, I have had to suspend exactly one student. We all know about the incident that led to that suspension, and no, we will not be stopping at any lemonade stand near any fireworks outlet in Virginia *this* time. You will not embarrass yourselves, our school, or us. Got that?" The students nodded mutely.

Alicia felt it burbling up inside her—that irrepressible urge to say something. She fought it for a moment and then decided that her duty as a teacher superseded her duty as a girl who was trying to get a boy to like her.

"Of course we understand that it's developmentally appropriate for you to test boundaries," she said hastily. "It just wouldn't be right on this particular trip." The students tittered a little. Typical Ms. Deats.

"Everybody stay quiet," Brian snapped. "Ms. Deats, may I have a word with you?"

"Of course," she said, wishing she hadn't said anything.

Brian crossed the aisle and bent his head to whisper in her ear.

"Can you do me a favor?" he said softly.

"Sure," she said, the top of her head tingling at how close he was. "Anything. Of course."

"Do not undermine me in front of the students," he said.

"I didn't mean to—" she said, but he was already back to lecturing the students.

"The trip to D.C. takes three hours," he said. "We won't stop between here and D.C."

"But what if I have to pee?" Kaylee whined. The other cheerleaders on the bus nodded vigorously. Kaylee was the cheer captain—a real feat for a sophomore, but she was very talented—and she possessed a notoriously small bladder. The cheerleaders were used to pulling over on the way to away games so that Kaylee could pee in a gas station or rest stop. Privately, they thought it was kind of funny, but they would never say so in front of their leader—and definitely not in front of her BFFs and co-rulers of the entire school.

"Obviously, if you can't hold it, we will pull over, Kaylee." Brian sighed.

"I mean, I have a medical issue," Kaylee said. "My mother is a doctor and she wrote a note that says . . ."

"We know about your mother's notes, Kaylee," Brian said. "She has sent me several over the years. I am well aware of your condition and if it proves to be a problem, you let us know and we will pull over at a rest stop."

"Good," Kaylee said. "Because I have a note. From a doctor. Who is my mother."

Brian nodded wearily and dropped into his seat. Alicia sat across the aisle from him, nervously wringing her hands together. The bus lurched into action, and as they turned out of the parking lot, Alicia wondered if she should bother apologizing, and if she did apologize, what she'd say, exactly, and if she'd be apologizing just for stepping on his authority today or if she could work in an apology about the thing after Chili's.

Oh, God. The thing after Chili's.

Alicia was a first-year teacher at Flemington High School, and she'd been really nervous at the introductory faculty mixer back in August. It was held at Chili's, which Alicia thought was kind of ridiculous when you considered there were some actual great independently owned and operated establishments in the area, but whatever. And everyone wore these stupid name tags, and Alicia drew a heart and a smiley face on hers but didn't write her name, because she thought that might be a fun and unusual way to start a conversation. (It had worked at her RA training her senior year at Hampshire. Of course, there were only 10 RAs at Hampshire, and there were 40 faculty and staff members at this mixer.) Anyway, nobody seemed to respond to her eager smile and abundant use of eye contact, so she gave up and nursed a gigantic margarita in the corner at a table by herself. She was fairly certain it was made with high fructose corn syrup, but she needed something in a pinch, and the margarita jumped out at her on the menu. She was staring down into its electric blue depths, wondering exactly what kinds of terrible chemicals she was ingesting, when she heard someone clear their throat.

"Excuse me," a voice said. "Is this seat taken?"

Alicia looked up, confused, and her eyes widened. For standing there, his head framed in the glow of a big-screen bar TV, was the most handsome man Alicia had seen in—well, maybe ever. At least since she had met her college boyfriend, Pendragon, whose real name was Arthur and had blond dreadlocks. He'd dropped out midway through junior year in order to manage an organic lavender farm in Vermont. This guy, with his dark hair and perfect cheekbones and glasses, was even more gorgeous than Pendragon/Arthur. He looked like Clark Kent. He was holding a glass of water.

"Well, is it?" the man asked solemnly. He seemed nervous.

"Is what?" Alicia asked dreamily.

He cleared his throat.

"Is this seat taken?" he asked.

"Oh!" Alicia said. "Oh, no, it's—it's not taken." As he sank into the chair, she zeroed in on his name tag. In neat capital letters, he had written MR. KENNER.

"Mr. Kenner," she said aloud. "Do you have a first name, like the rest of us?"

"Said the woman with the smiley face and the heart on her name tag," he observed dryly. Alicia looked down and laughed.

"I'm Alicia," she said, holding out her hand.

"Brian," he said, shaking her hand. He looked around the restaurant and sighed.

"Don't you hate these things?" Brian said. "They're so boring."

"This is my first one," Alicia said. "I'm new."

"Oh," Brian said. "I never know who's new and who isn't."

"Don't you know who your co-workers are?" Alicia asked. It was a pretty small school, after all—about 60 students in each grade.

"I know who my students are," Brian said. "That's all that matters. I try not to get too involved with my co-workers. They come and go." He glanced at her briefly before turning his gaze downward to his phone. He was texting—or so she thought; she couldn't really see the screen.

It seemed kind of rude.

"What do you teach?" Alicia asked.

"What?" he said.

"What subject do you teach?"

"Oh. Math," he said, and returned to his phone.

This was like pulling teeth. Really aloof teeth.

"What grades?"

"Huh?"

"What grades do you teach?"

"All grades," he said. "All levels, including AP Calc."

"Wow," Alicia said, impressed. "That's amazing."

"Not really," he said, and for a moment she thought he blushed. But then, in the blink of an eye, he was back to doing whatever he was doing on his phone.

"To me it's pretty amazing," Alicia tried again. "I suck at math."

"I'm guessing you don't teach math, then," he said, not taking his eyes off his phone.

"Social studies," Alicia said. "Contemporary World Studies, History. I'm hoping they'll let me teach Honors History eventually, but I think veteran teachers get first pick."

"We do," Brian said.

"Ah," Alicia said lamely. She signaled the waiter for another margarita.

A full two minutes of silence went by, which is awful when you're in a Chili's and you're mildly intoxicated and you're not sure exactly why the incredibly cute guy with the perfect cheekbones is staring at his phone instead of you. By the time Alicia got a refill on her margarita, she was miserable enough to say something, anything.

"Texting your girlfriend?" Alicia blurted out. She hadn't meant to say *that*. She drank more of her margarita.

"That's kind of personal," Brian said. Was he blushing? He was blushing. At any rate, he looked uncomfortable.

"Oh, I'm sorry," Alicia said. "I didn't mean to offend you."

"I don't have a girlfriend," Brian said.

"Well, neither do I," Alicia said brightly.

Brian looked at her for a moment, and then he did something that surprised her. He slid his phone across the table to her. Confused, she looked at the screen, which was a jumble of numbers and symbols.

"It's an app," he said. "One of my student mathletes designed it over the summer. I'm beta-testing it."

"Wh-what does it do?" Alicia asked.

At this, Brian's eyes brightened. "Well, it's fairly simple," he began, and then proceeded to speak uninterrupted for four minutes about stuff that befuddled Alicia. She nodded along, wishing she had paid more attention in math in high school, or middle school, or ever. Here and there she recognized a term or two, but the truth was that Alicia's life didn't require much math beyond basic arithmetic. This was true of most adults she knew, actually, but she wasn't about to say *that*, not when Brian was finally warming up.

He paused, and looked at her curiously. "Am I making sense?" he asked, a little shyly.

"No," she answered. "But I really like listening to you talk." Oh, wow. Yep, that was the second margarita kicking in.

Brian looked at her for a moment, and then he did something really great.

He *laughed*.

It was a real laugh, one of genuine amusement, as if he were actually tickled by what she'd said.

"You're funny," he said, and it sounded like he meant it. "And I'm—a dork. Sorry. I have like, major social anxiety. I don't know why I just told you that." He immediately looked embarrassed.

"Well, I'm mildly intoxicated," Alicia said, even though the truth was she was beyond "mildly intoxicated" at this point. She could handle marijuana fairly well, but alcohol was another story altogether.

"Oh, you are?" he said, concerned. "You aren't driving home, are you?"

Oh, shit. She'd forgotten about the whole "driving home" thing.

"I guess I'll just sit here until I'm sober," she said finally.

"You're tiny, and those margaritas are huge," Brian said. "That could take a while."

"Fuck," Alicia said, a little loudly, and then clapped her hand over her mouth.

Brian seemed amused. "We're allowed to swear, you know," he said. "There are no kids here."

Alicia sank into her seat. "I'm just so embarrassed," she said. "I'm drunk. Like I'm actually drunk. And it's my first faculty—thing, ever. Oh my God. What if the principal catches me?"

"How old are you, exactly?" Brian asked. He didn't sound mean.

"Twenty-three," Alicia said. "I'm too old to get drunk at a work party."

"I don't know," Brian said. "I don't think you're the only one. You're just the youngest one." He jerked his thumb in the direction of a clique of English teachers who were screaming with laughter at some joke one of them had made. They all appeared to be in their fifties and sixties, at least. And they all appeared to be pretty toasted.

"Teachers drink," Brian said. "A lot."

"Not you," Alicia said. "Unless that's a giant glass of vodka."

"Drinking's not for me," Brian said.

"I'm usually like that," Alicia said quickly. "I really don't drink that much ever. That's why I'm like this right now. I'm not used to it. I just smoke weed."

"You might not want to say that too loudly," Brian said.

"Am I talking loudly?" Alicia said, loudly.

"Yes," Brian said, laughing again.

"Oh, shit," Alicia whispered. She knocked over her margarita with her elbow, and Brian jumped up to wipe the table with a napkin.

"I am so sorry," Alicia said.

"Maybe it's time for you to go home," Brian suggested. He stood up abruptly.

"Oh, sorry," Alicia said. "Bye, I guess." She waved at him. He just stood there.

"Aren't you going?" Alicia said.

"No, I'm taking *you* home," Brian said.

"Oh, that makes more sense," Alicia said. She stood up and wobbled. "I should say bye to the principal first!"

"No," Brian said. "No, you really shouldn't. And you definitely shouldn't drive. Cops have nothing to do in this town. They love to pull people over."

"You're very smart," Alicia said, and followed him out of the restaurant.

His car was immaculate, and Alicia clambered into the front seat, inhaling that new car smell.

"When did you get this?" she asked him as they both buckled themselves in.

"Six years ago," he said.

"Oh my God, you're so *clean*," she said. "My car is like this total landfill."

They were driving before she knew it. He asked where she lived, and she told him. They were maybe six minutes away, so there wasn't much time for in-depth conversation, but Alicia kept up a steady stream of chatter about everything: her excitement about the coming school year; her nervousness about being a good teacher; the Buddha statue she'd just bought at a "sacred objects" shop in New Hope and hoped to put in the classroom if it was okay with her supervisor; how much she missed her Hampshire friends; and nearly anything else that came to mind. Brian drove silently, and she couldn't tell if he was actually paying any attention to her or not, but in her drunken state she resolved that if only she spoke *more*, he would inevitably start to find her interesting. They pulled up in front of her apartment.

"This it?" Brian asked.

"This what?"

"Your place."

"Oh. Oh! Yes! That's my apartment! Oh my God, it's so cute. Do you want to see it?" She grinned at him. He was so nice, even though he was obviously a total dork. She liked dorks. Always had.

He smiled at her. "I would if we didn't have that all-faculty meeting at 9 tomorrow morning," he said. "Besides, you're probably tired of talking to the old boring math guy."

"How old are you?" Alicia asked.

"Twenty-nine," he said.

"That's barely even old," Alicia said, laughing.

He laughed. "Thanks for the compliment, kiddo." He paused and appeared to be struggling internally with something. Then he took a deep breath and said, "I like listening to you talk. I really do. Maybe we could talk again sometime."

"I could talk to you for hours and hours," she said, putting her hand on his thigh. She leaned in and kissed him. Then she pulled back and clapped her hand over her mouth.

"I am so sorry," she said.

Brian grinned at her and leaned in and kissed her.

"Me too," he said.

She kissed him again.

"This is totally inappropriate," she said.

He kissed her back.

"Yeah this is awful," he said.

She kissed him again, and this time she bit his lip a little.

"Is this easing your social anxiety?" she asked.

He kissed her back, and this time he pulled her hair a little.

"I don't know. We probably need to do it a few more times before I can give you a verdict."

And then they were making out, and it was totally hot, and Alicia was having the best time she'd had in years. Like, *years*. Maybe it was because he was a few years older and therefore vastly more mature than the college boys she'd made out with at Hampshire. At any rate, it was fucking awesome, even if she was increasingly dizzy. She put her hand on his thigh, and he was immediately hard, and she actually said out loud, "Fuck it," and he laughed and she unzipped his pants and pulled out his dick and started jerking him off.

"Oh my God," Brian moaned, closing his eyes. "You're amazing."

"Thank you," Alicia said.

And that's just about when she puked all over his crotch.

"Oh my God!" Brian gasped, opening the door to his car and hopping out. He did a kind of spastic dance, which would've been funny if he hadn't been doing it in order to shake Alicia's puke off his penis.

"Oh God!" he said, as Alicia shakily got out of the car and ran around to his side. "This is—oh my God. There's puke on my dick. Like, on my actual dick."

"I'm so sorry!" Alicia shrieked, trying hard not to cry. "Oh my Gooood. I'm so sorry. Wait, I can help!" She pulled up her long, organic cotton skirt and tried to wipe some of her vomit off the crotch of his pants.

"No, you don't have to do that!" he said quickly, backing away and zipping up. "Oh, God, it's squishy."

She tripped and fell in the street.

"Are you okay?" he said. "Aw, Jesus, Alicia." He gingerly helped her to her feet.

She stood up as straight as she could, ignoring the scrape on her knee. She was going to fix this. She was going to make it okay.

"Do you want to come inside?" she asked, her voice tinged with hysteria. "I can clean off your pants. I have a washer dryer. You can take a shower. You can wear a blanket while you wait for your clothes. I have a really comfortable throw. It's an afghan. It's actually from this women's collective in Afghanistan so it's like literally an afghan."

"I should go home," Brian said. "I'm sorry, I just—I have this thing with puke. Like it really grosses me out. I'm so sorry. It's kind of a phobia. It's why I can't have a dog. Do you have your keys?"

"Yes," Alicia wailed, producing them from her little woven hemp purse. "They're right here!" She held them up in front of his face.

"Um, okay," Brian said. "I'm gonna—okay . . . I'll, um— see you tomorrow. This . . . let's just . . . this never happened. Okay?"

"Okay," Alicia said, trying really hard not to cry in front of him.

And he got in his no-longer-immaculate car and roared off down the street, leaving her standing by the curb, her knee starting to bleed a little, her face crumpled. She cried all the way up to her bed, where she fell asleep in a heap. When she woke up, there was dried vomit crusted on the hem of her skirt, where she'd wiped some of it off his pants.

That was nine months ago, in August. He'd not spoken a word to her since, unless you counted the occasional nod and pained smile when she said hello in the hallway. She'd thought about him often, particularly since she passed him every day on her walk from third period to the faculty lounge. He was even handsomer than she'd realized when she met him at Chili's, and she couldn't bear to think that their only real interaction would be that night. It was just too embarrassing to contemplate, and besides, she'd felt like they had a real connection, maybe, for a moment, before she blew chunks all over his junk. She knew his reputation as a stickler, a really tough teacher who brooked zero insubordination from his students, but she knew he must love them, too. She could just tell. And if he'd only give her another shot—if he'd only talk to her, or even make full eye contact, maybe she could make things right.

But Brian Kenner seemed utterly, completely, and totally uninterested in Alicia Deats. Clearly, she had used up whatever chance she'd had with him, and she wouldn't get another one. Alicia thought about that night every single day at work, every time she passed Brian or heard a student complain about what a hardass Mr. Kenner could be.

It wasn't the only thing she thought about, of course. She loved her job immediately and adored her homeroom full of sophomores (she would never have said she had a favorite, but she had a special fondness for little Gertie Santanello-Smith. What a sweet kid. Just needed to spread her wings a little.) Every class section was new and different and challenging and amazing in some way. She even managed to make a few friends in the social studies department, and bonded with one of the gym teachers, Patti Bump, who brought her in to teach yoga once a week. (Alicia didn't realize that the boys in the class greeted her so enthusiastically because her butt looked so cute in yoga pants, or that Patti Bump also enjoyed the view, but that was probably for the best.) As a first-year teacher, she was constantly busy, constantly trying to figure out how to manage her time, constantly trying to navigate the occasionally confusing political waters of a public high school. But with the help of Patti Bump and the other social studies teachers, she found her way. She even found a nice group to sit with in the faculty lounge during lunch.

But there were moments—like when she passed him in that hallway, or heard his name—that Alicia thought about Brian and felt a mixture of anxiety, embarrassment, and longing.

So when the principal announced at a faculty meeting that they would need one more chaperone for the sophomore D.C. trip "to help Mr. Kenner out," Alicia's hand shot up as if she were an eager teen herself. The other teachers chuckled good-naturedly—except for Brian, they were all older than Alicia by at least a decade, and found her youthful energy to be entertaining.

"Yes, Alicia?" the principal said, amused. "I love that you raised your hand."

Alicia hadn't realized that she had raised her hand. She lowered it sheepishly.

"Um," she said. "It's just—I love Washington, D.C. I've been there a few times."

"Ah, for peace and love marches?" said the principal teasingly. The principal was a Republican and got a kick out of Alicia's liberal leanings, even when some of the parents didn't.

"Well, and climate change protests," Alicia said. "Anyway, I'd love to help Mr. Kenner—Brian—I'd love to help Brian out." She looked at him hopefully and he studiously avoided her gaze.

"It's like watching Bambi," one of the teachers whispered to the other, and Alicia overheard, but she didn't care.

"Well, Brian," the principal said with a smile. "It looks like you've got yourself a partner. May the Lord protect you both from the evils that teens do."

Brian did not look pleased. He opened his mouth to speak, and then seemed to think better of it. He nodded his assent.

And that's how Alicia ended up on that bus, wondering if she and Brian would get to spend any time alone. School protocol dictated that chaperones on trips figure out twenty-four-hour coverage for student safety, meaning someone had to be up at any given hour, prepared for disaster. Patti Bump and the social studies teachers had assured Alicia that none of the teachers actually adhered to the rule, and that everybody deserved a good rest after a day chasing the monsters all around a museum or a landmark or whatever, and if the kids got up to some shenanigans in the wee hours, well, it was no problem so long as they didn't get themselves hurt or arrested. Alicia got the distinct feeling Brian would not have approved of that laissez-faire policy, and that she and he would stick to school protocol.

Alicia looked over at Brian, and he met her gaze. She smiled hopefully, and he hesitated for a moment before nodding politely. Then he looked away from her, out the window. Deflated, she sank back into the uncomfortable faux-leather seat.

There had to be a way to get through to him.

But how?

Near the back of the bus, seated out of earshot of the teachers, Gertie was listening to "Kids in America" by The Muffs. It's a 1995 cover of a 1981 Kim Wilde song, and it's amazing. The lyrics are all about being bored in suburbia, so Gertie, born in China and quickly adopted by parents in tiny-ass Flemington, could totally relate. Her mom always asked, "What's this song about? Is it about drugs?" whenever she played any music at all, but Gertie was pretty sure "Kids in America" had nothing to do with drugs. Or if it did, it was only tangentially related to drug use. The song was about wanting to party, and Gertie was well aware that for some of her fellow sophomores, partying meant getting high. Not for her, though. She'd never done drugs. Rachel, her best friend—she was another story. Even Sivan smoked pot sometimes, but she got straight A's so it obviously didn't hurt her at all.

Gertie's dad always said, "Gertie, we trust you completely. It's these other kids we're not so sure about." They didn't mean Rachel and Sivan, of course—they meant strangers, kids they didn't know. The imaginary big bad wolf that was always hovering on the edge of every experience. Rachel once said to Gertie that it must be because she was their only child—and adopted at that—and Gertie tended to agree. Rachel could be insightful about human behavior. She wasn't just book-smart.

Rachel once remarked how interesting it was that Gertie, who was born in China, did a bunch of Italian Catholic stuff on Christmas Eve as per her mother's traditions—the Feast of the Seven Fishes—whereas Sivan, who was Jewish, ate Chinese food every Christmas Day.

"That's actually not very interesting, Rachel," Sivan had said. "You just think Jews are special because at church they told you we're like magical elves or something." Sivan loved to tease Rachel about her crazy church, where they offered "conversion therapy" for homosexuals.

"I believe exactly zero percent of what they say in my church and you know it," said Rachel.

"I mean, real Chinese food isn't even like the stuff we eat here," Sivan said, rubbing the back of her short dark hair like she always did. Sivan had actually been to China. She had been all over the world with her parents. Even Rachel had traveled on mission trips to faraway places with her family.

Gertie had nothing to add, because not only had she not been to China since she was an infant, she had not been *anywhere* interesting, really, unless you counted the Canadian side of Niagara Falls, which she did not. A social worker mom and a therapist dad didn't exactly make enough for vacations to anywhere but the Jersey Shore and, once, Disney World. And it wasn't like Gertie was going off and having adventures on her own.

It wasn't that Gertie was uptight. Sure, she didn't do drugs, but that wasn't a measure of how cool someone was. And okay, so she'd never actually kissed a boy, which objectively speaking was awful, but even that could probably wait till junior year or even senior year if absolutely necessary. It's more that Gertie was average in many ways: average height, average weight, average attractiveness. Being born in another country was maybe the only interesting thing about Gertie. You wouldn't notice her if you walked past her on the street.

At least, that's what she thought.

Anyway, "Kids in America." Gertie loved that song. It opened with a kind of controlled anticipatory tension before exploding into unbridled fun. Gertie herself spent a lot of time in controlled anticipatory tension and not a whole lot of time having unbridled fun.

When Gertie was listening to "Kids in America," she was going through Instagram, because if there was one thing Gertie really loved besides her best friends and '90s music, it was photography. Her father had always told her, "Never be a lawyer or an artist—the first is evil but you'll eat well; the second is good but you'll eat nothing." Her parents didn't make a whole lot of money, so Gertie was looking for a job that would help her sock away funds for a real camera. Jobs in town were few and far between, though.

It wasn't like her parents were so excited for her to get a camera, either. One time Gertie broached the subject that maybe she might like to take some fine arts courses in college. Her father frowned.

"But it's nothing you'd want to do for a career," Gertie's mom said, without even asking Gertie what she thought. Gertie's mom and dad rarely, if ever, asked Gertie what she thought.

"I don't know," Gertie said, feeling emboldened. "I love taking photos. People say I'm good at it. Maybe I could be a photographer."

"A photographer." Her father snorted. "Come on, Gertie. Of what?"

"I don't know," Gertie said again, because she really didn't (although she loved photographing food, but she knew her parents would laugh at that). She fumbled for a response and seized on the first true thing that came to mind.

"Beautiful things," she said.

"You want a career photographing . . . beautiful things?" her mother asked, looking over her reading glasses with some mixture of surprise and dismay.

"No, she doesn't," Gertie's father said, smiling kindly at her. He reached over and patted Gertie on the head, like he always did whenever she said something he deemed silly. "She wants to be a therapist or a social worker or a teacher . . . something that's always needed. Something that doesn't go in and out of fashion."

Gertie knew she didn't want to be a social worker or a therapist. And as soon as she'd told her parents she wanted to be a photographer, she got a sudden feeling she'd never felt before. It was like a shock of recognition, but it wasn't in her brain, it was in her stomach. Maybe that's what people called a gut feeling.

Whatever it was, it said, "Bingo!"

The conversation with her parents was a couple weeks before the day Gertie listened to "Kids in America" and aimlessly scrolled through Instagram, but it was still in the back of her mind. Was she going to end up doing exactly what her parents wanted all the time, or would she figure something else out? Something different and fascinating and exciting?

A new photo popped up in Gertie's feed.

It was a picture of Danny Bryan . . .

. . . at the Vietnam War Memorial in Washington, D.C.

And Gertie almost fell over.

First things first: Gertie was not logged into her regular Instagram account, but her anonymous Instagram account. She had created the anonymous account the previous summer specifically so she could follow one person: Danny Bryan. For appearance's sake, the anonymous account followed various other accounts—celebrities, randoms who took good photos, whatever. But the whole point was to keep track of the life and times of Danny Bryan.

Danny was a fellow counselor at the sleepaway camp in the New Jersey Pine Barrens where Gertie had been going for a month every summer since she was nine. The only reason her parents could afford the luxury of camp was that the camp director was an old grad school friend of Gertie's dad's, and he always cut Gertie's parents a nice deal. Danny Bryan was a certified lifeguard. He played lacrosse. He could sing and play guitar, and he had floppy brown hair that got in his eyes, and he was particularly beloved by the youngest campers, and he was perfect.

Unfortunately, he did not go to Flemington High School. At the moment, Danny Bryan was a senior at Lindbergh High School, which was a half-hour drive and a world away. People at FHS didn't mix with people at Lindbergh, and people at Lindbergh didn't mix with people at FHS. They were major football rivals, lacrosse rivals, everything rivals. Even the mathletes at FHS hated the mathletes at Lindbergh. The two debate teams always ended up in the state finals, and people in Flemington who knew nothing about debate actually gave a shit about this simply because it meant "we can beat Lindbergh." It all sounded stupid to Gertie. But she cared about it because Danny Bryan went to Lindbergh.

Gertie had noticed Danny Bryan when she was nine and he was eleven. It was the summer after third grade, her first time at camp, and she was nervous about being away from her parents for an entire month.

On the trip down to camp, Gertie's mother waxed rhapsodic about archery lessons and color wars and canoeing and camping out under the stars—all the things she had loved at her own summer camp many years before. Her father was excited that Gertie, who was a little bit of an indoor kid, would spend time running around in the sun, "although of course you've got to be sure to wear SPF 30 or higher every single day, Gertie."

"And a hat," her mother had chimed in.

"Skin cancer is a serious concern," her father had said.

"Okay," Gertie had said.

When they got to camp, a group of older boys was assembled near the entrance. They were laughing and goofing around, knocking each other's baseball caps off and giving each other wedgies. Gertie's dad drove slowly through the entrance, being careful not to hit an errant camper, and Gertie stared at the boys in wonder. Then there came the sound of a strange clattering behind them.

"HEY!" came a voice. "SIR! EXCUSE ME! SIR!"

Gertie's dad hit the brakes and peered at the young boy running up behind them. Gertie stared at him out the back windshield. The closer he got, the more beautiful he became. He finally reached the driver's side window and held out a dusty tin rectangle.

"Your license plate, sir," he said. "It fell off back there."

His eyes flickered to the backseat briefly, and he gave Gertie a friendly smile like any well-behaved kid would give the small daughter of a stranger.

This was Danny Bryan.

And that was it.

Gertie was gone. Done for. Just like that, she'd met the boy she knew would be the love of her entire life. At nine years old, Gertie was hopelessly smitten.

A few days later, in the mess hall, Gertie mustered up the courage to talk to Danny Bryan. She approached him near the salad bar, where he was piling leafy greens on his plate—the only kid at camp who did that of his own accord, probably.

"Hi," she said, staring up at him.

"Hi," he said, looking at her quizzically.

She realized then he had no idea who she was. The feeling socked her in the gut like a closed fist.

"Bye," she said, and walked away.

That was the last conversation she had with him. There were four hundred campers, divided into groups by age, and for the next four summers, Gertie watched longingly from afar as Danny Bryan grew into exactly the kind of gorgeous being who drives pre-adolescent girls to distraction—and adolescent girls to wild fits of moaning and writhing. Gertie preferred to silently moan and softly writhe while she thought about Danny Bryan, particularly when she was masturbating and thinking about him, something she had started doing when she was ten and learned about masturbation from some 1970s book called *The Young Womyn's Guide To Growing Up*. She found it in the attic while looking for her mother's *Free to Be You and Me* record. The book had illustrations of different kinds of breasts and vaginas and bellies and butts and it said that female bodies were a beautiful wonderland that should be cherished and celebrated. It didn't have instructions for masturbation, exactly, but it explained what it *was*, and since Gertie hadn't previously known it was even a thing, she felt the need to explore on her own. It soon became her favorite private activity, though she never discussed it with Rachel and Sivan or, ew, her parents.

Once, Rachel brightly brought up masturbation in ninth grade health class when they were discussing healthy alternatives to sex. Everyone laughed, but Rachel didn't seem fazed in the least. Gertie blushed and pretended to focus on the cover of her notebook, where she was doodling Danny Bryan's name in purple felt-tip marker.

"That is an alternative to sexual intercourse, Rachel," their health and gym teacher, Ms. Bump, said encouragingly. "But it's not something we discuss in our curriculum."

"I just think every girl in the world should get a vibrator as soon as she turns fourteen," Rachel said in that same sweet, weirdly innocent voice. Across the room, Sivan sighed loudly and stared at the ceiling.

"Well, that's definitely not something we'll discuss in class," Ms. Bump said. "That's a . . . family conversation."

"Not my family," Rachel said. She grinned and winked at Gertie, and Gertie turned redder. Rachel could really push the envelope sometimes, but she always got away with it because she was so pretty and so sweet.

Then later in the cafeteria lunch line, like some kind of psychic with no emotional boundaries, Rachel turned around and smiled conspiratorially at Gertie.

"*You* know what I meant today in class," she said.

"About what?" Gertie said, playing dumb.

"Oh, come *on*," Rachel said, giggling. "I bet he's great, too."

"Who?"

"Danny Bryan. In your fantasies. While you totally masturbate." She said it loudly enough that other people could hear.

Sivan, who was vegan and only got in the lunch line to accompany her friends, poked Rachel in the arm.

"You're embarrassing Gertie," she whispered.

"I am liberating Gertie," Rachel said. "I'm freeing her from the shackles of a society that doesn't understand a woman's sexuality."

"Have you been reading that feminist website again?" Sivan groaned.

"What, like you're not a feminist?"

"Of course I'm a feminist," Sivan said. "I'm a queer intersectional feminist, duh. I just don't feel like talking about vibrators in health class is appropriate."

"What*ever*," Rachel sang. "I'm a sex-positive feminist."

"You don't even know what that means," Sivan said.

"I mostly do," Rachel said. "It means you think sex is cool."

"You've never even had sex," Sivan said.

"Of course I haven't!" Rachel said indignantly. "I'm waiting till I'm sixteen, duh." (In fact, she DID go on to wait until she was sixteen. Rachel was good at sticking to promises.)

Gertie got out of the lunch line and hid in the girls' bathroom for the rest of the period. She did not masturbate. There was nothing as unsexy as a public school bathroom.

Anyway, there is no way to overestimate the incredible, momentous importance of the instant Gertie realized that Danny Bryan was in Washington, D.C., the day before she was scheduled to go to Washington, D.C. She looked at the photo again, just to make sure she wasn't dreaming. The time stamp said it had been taken an hour ago. This time, she read the caption.

"Saw my uncle's name on the wall. Amazing. Never thought a class trip could be like this. Hopefully next few days in D.C. are just as incredible."

Next.

Few.

Days.

Next few days!

HOLY SHIT.

Danny Bryan was going to be in Washington, D.C. for the next few *fucking* days!

Gertie couldn't handle it. Her heart was pounding. Her hands were sweating. She did not know what to do with herself. So she did the only thing that seemed do able in that moment: she punched Rachel in the shoulder.

"Ow!" Rachel yelped, thankfully not loud enough for the teachers to hear her. She pulled out her earbuds and stared at Gertie. "Gertie, what the fuck?"

Wordlessly, Gertie handed her the phone and pointed.

"Oh, shit," Rachel said, immediately grasping the importance of the situation. "Are you fucking kidding me? He's in D.C. too?" She poked Sivan and showed her the phone.

"Good old Danny Bryan," Sivan said. For the past seven years, they'd been hearing about Danny Bryan and seeing photos of Danny Bryan and scheming how Gertie could talk to Danny Bryan. Sivan was very familiar with the boy's visage, and while she didn't personally find him attractive, she could understand why Gertie was into him.

Gertie refreshed Danny Bryan's Instagram feed, and a new photo popped up from just a few seconds ago! It was a photograph of the outside of the United States Holocaust Memorial Museum. The caption read: "Feeling overwhelmed as we get ready to go in here."

"Fuck!" Gertie snapped, just loud enough for kids in the surrounding rows to take notice and stare at her.

"You scared me," Sivan said.

"Be patient with her," Rachel said. "She is in love."

"She is not in love," Sivan said. "She is infatuated."

"Well, how would you know what being in love is like?" Rachel asked. "I know I haven't been in love. And I know you've never been in love, except maybe with Angelina Jolie in that one movie."

"*Gia*," Sivan said automatically. "It was her break-through performance."

"You just like it because she totally does it with a girl," Rachel said.

"The acting is excellent," Sivan said primly.

Gertie couldn't take their back-and-forth. Not right now.

"Can we focus, please?" Gertie demanded. "Look!" She showed the Instagram to Sivan and Rachel.

"Oh, now he's at the Holocaust Museum," Sivan said. "Well, I'm glad it's affecting him deeply. It should. It's a living memorial to the greatest evil the world has ever seen. Although of course we can't discount the atrocities taking place even today . . ."

Gertie looked at Rachel.

"Sivan," Rachel said. "He's at the Holocaust Museum right now. That's where we're headed."

"Maybe we'll see him there," Sivan said, shrugging. Sivan had been to the U.S. Holocaust Memorial Museum more times than she could count. Her grandfather had been on the planning committee. It was a very special place and a very sad place and she didn't exactly relish going there, but she regarded it as an important experience for everyone and she really hoped their less sensitive classmates would be respectful.

"No, we won't see him there," Gertie said. "So we've got, what, two and a half hours left on this drive?"

"About that, yeah," Sivan said.

"Meaning we will probably just miss him," Gertie said with enormous disappointment. "We could've seen him. We could've been at the museum at the exact same time as him and we could've seen him."

"You could've talked to him," Rachel said sympathetically. "I totally get it."

"Um, what exactly would you have said at the Holocaust Museum?" Sivan asked, trying hard not to actually yell at them. She loved them, but they could be super-dense sometimes about anything social or political or historical or, well, important.

"I don't know," Gertie said glumly. "I probably wouldn't have said anything. I get so shy around him."

"You're kind of shy around everybody," Sivan pointed out.

"Sivan!" Rachel said. "Encourage her!"

"To what? Hit on some bro at the Holocaust Museum?" Sivan was indignant. "That's so gross."

"Have you seen *The Fault in Our Stars*?" Rachel asked. "They made out at the Anne Frank House and it was totally inspiring."

"*The Fault in Our Stars* was ridiculous," Sivan said, her voice rising. "It was the stupidest movie I've ever seen!" At this, a hush fell over the girls seated nearby. From a few rows away, Peighton, Brooklynn, and Kaylee turned around and glared, as did most of the girls nearby.

"What?" snapped Olivia Alvarez from across the aisle.

"Are you serious?" said her seatmate, Kaitlynne Bronson.

"Only a monster wouldn't like *The Fault in Our Stars*," Peighton said loudly.

"Exactly," said Olivia and Kaitlynne in unison.

Peighton folded her arms and smirked.

"Are we having this conversation?" Sivan said to Rachel and Gertie. "Is this actually happening?"

"No one asked you," Rachel sweetly said to Peighton.

"Don't talk to us," Brooklynn snapped.

Rachel's smile grew wider. "I'm sorry," she said. "I couldn't hear you over the sound of my hair growing." She waved her middle finger in the air and then flipped her long blond hair with it.

"Is he the only boy you haven't blown?" Brooklynn asked, pointing at Sivan. Sivan shrank into herself. Gertie put a protective hand on her arm.

"No, that's Brock Chuddford," Rachel said. "But don't worry. I will." Brock Chuddford was the handsomest boy in

the sophomore class. He was sitting up front right behind
Mr. Kenner, because he wasn't allowed to sit with his
friends in the back, because he always ended up "rough-
housing," as Mr. Kenner put it. Brock Chuddford had been
Brooklynn's boyfriend freshman year. He was incredibly
good-looking and popular, and he had dumped Brooklynn
at a school dance because she was taking time away from
his focus on lacrosse. Everyone had seen it happen and
had witnessed Brooklynn's subsequent screaming rage fit,
which had required faculty intervention in the form of Ms.
Bump dragging her to the office and calling her parents to
pick her up. And though nobody would dare bring it up,
everybody knew Brooklynn's parents had made her go to
a psychiatrist for a good six months after her freakout, because the school had strongly recommended it. Brooklynn
was so obsessed with Brock Chuddford to this day that
the school always made sure they had no classes together.
So basically, by even speaking Brock Chuddford's name,
Rachel was bringing up the very worst wound Brooklynn
had ever suffered—and throwing salt in it. Plus, like, hot
sauce and lemon juice. And piss. And acid.

"You fucking bitch!" Brooklynn hissed, starting to get
up from her seat. Peighton, the athlete, pulled her down
while Kaylee shot devil eyes at Gertie. Ms. Deats noticed
the commotion and called out, "Is everything all right,
girls?" Mr. Kenner's head snapped around and he glared
at them. Even Brock Chuddford's head turned around,

but when he saw it had to do with Brooklynn, he quickly looked away. He was a little scared of her. Everybody was.

"Everything's fine," Rachel called back. "We're just so excited to get to D.C.!"

"You girls," Ms. Deats said fondly. "I love the enthusiasm. But stay calm now. You're going to need your energy for three days of active learning!"

Brooklynn, Peighton, Kaylee, Rachel, Sivan, and Gertie smiled tightly and nodded. Mr. Kenner stared suspiciously at each of them in turn before resuming his study of whatever was going on outside the window.

"This isn't over," Brooklynn mouthed to Rachel.

"I'm sorry, I can't hear you," Rachel said. "Can you speak into this microphone?" She raised her middle finger again and tapped it. "Testing, testing . . . is this thing on? Gertie, can you talk into it and check?" She held it under Gertie's mouth.

"Just wait," Kaylee hissed. "We're gonna do something in D.C."

"I love when that one speaks," Rachel said loudly to Sivan. "Isn't it adorable when it has thoughts?"

"Oh my God, Rachel," Sivan muttered, staring out the window. "You are not helping to defuse the situation."

Brooklynn, Peighton, and Kaylee put their heads together and whispered. Sivan looked over nervously and caught Peighton's eye. Peighton smiled slowly, like the Grinch.

Well, this couldn't be good.

"We should totally sneak out tonight and find Danny Bryan," Rachel whispered to Sivan and Gertie. "It'll be so fun!"

"That's absurd," Sivan said. "Right, Gertie? Tell her it's absurd."

Gertie thought for a moment.

"Of course it's absurd," she said, and grew very quiet. Sivan and Rachel could tell she was deep in thought.

When the bus entered D.C., Alicia looked at Brian. It was that time, and they both knew it.

"Do you want to tell them, or should I?" Alicia said.

"Better if it's me," Brian said. "You'd probably apologize to them."

Alicia felt mildly insulted. "Excuse me," she said. "I would not. I would simply explain to them that in the context of this particular trip, with the focus on learning, it makes sense for them to—"

"Hand over your cell phones!" Mr. Kenner said in his booming, this-means-business voice.

The students stared at him in abject shock.

"Wh-what?" Olivia said, her lower lip quivering.

"But I need mine!" Gertie said, her voice hitting a slightly hysterical pitch. "I need mine because—because—I just do." Sivan and Rachel looked at her sympathetically.

"You can't be serious, dawg," Brock said.

"I can be incredibly serious, Brock, and calling me 'dawg' is your first strike," Mr. Kenner said. "School trip protocol says that no cell phones may be used except in an emergency."

"But nobody *ever* follows school trip protocol!" Kaitlynne whined. "Ms. Bump let us use our phones two weeks ago on our tour of the hospital!"

"I am not Ms. Bump," said Mr. Kenner. "I am Mr. Kenner. And I follow school protocol exactly."

"But what if we need to use Insta . . . I mean, what if our parents need to contact us?" Gertie asked with evident desperation.

"I just sent an email to all your parents reminding them of the rule," Mr. Kenner said. "They signed off on this rule when they signed your permission slips for this trip."

"No one actually reads the permission slips, though," Peighton grumbled.

"That's not my problem, Peighton," Mr. Kenner said. "They have my cell phone number if they need to get in touch. I'll have it on all day and all night. Now give me your phones." He pulled out a backpack and walked slowly up and down the aisle, collecting the now-contraband phones from the very, very, very unhappy students. Kaylee in particular looked as if she might burst into tears.

When Brian got back to the front of the bus, he handed over the backpack to Alicia.

"I assume I can trust you with this," he said without a hint of emotion or good humor.

"Obviously," she said testily, taking the backpack from him. She resented his flat tone, even if his eyes did twinkle in a really cute way. And those cheekbones . . .

"You know how this trip goes, but let's go over it one more time," Brian said, turning back to the students. "Today we're at the Holocaust Museum, then dinner, then we're at the hotel. Tomorrow we have breakfast at the hotel. Then we go to the National Museum of the American Indian, where we will eat lunch. This will be followed by the Air and Space Museum, and then dinner, and then the hotel. The next day is our last day. We will eat breakfast at the hotel, head to the White House, and then head home. Got it?"

"Got it," everybody said.

When they pulled up beside the Holocaust Memorial Museum, Brian told all the students that their luggage would stay on the bus.

"Just bring some money for the gift shop," Alicia said, loud and clear. She was tired of him taking the lead on this trip. "And any medication you may need. Carter, don't forget your inhaler." Carter Bump, Ms. Bump's pudgy, awkward, deeply asthmatic nephew, nodded.

"Let's go, team," Brian said, and looked at Alicia. "You ready?"

"Of course," she said, and followed him off the bus. She even believed it when she said it.

The students waited uncomfortably in the lobby of the museum as Mr. Kenner and Ms. Deats conferred with a staff member about their group reservation. Rachel gazed around the space with wide eyes. There were signs for exhibits on the Holocaust, the German invasion of Poland, the camp at Auschwitz, films and literature inspired by the Holocaust, and more. One sign in particular caught her attention.

"Why is there an exhibit on Rwanda?" she whispered to Sivan.

"Part of the museum's purpose is to educate people on other genocides that have happened since the Holocaust," Sivan said. "That was one of my grandfather's big things when he was on the planning commission."

"Wow," Rachel said quietly. "That's pretty cool. I mean, it's not *cool*. But you know what I mean."

"I know what you mean," Sivan said, smiling patiently.

"It's a Jewish thing, right?" Carter Bump asked from behind Gertie. Gertie, Sivan, and Rachel turned to look at him.

"Is what a Jewish thing?" Sivan asked suspiciously. She got a lot of weird and, to be honest, sometimes offensive questions from kids about her Judaism whenever a Jewish holiday rolled around. Flemington wasn't exactly a Jewish stronghold. Most of the kids were Catholic or Presbyterian. And dumb, not that their religion had anything to do with that. They just didn't seem to care about anything that happened outside the mall and the school hallways.

"Social justice," Carter said. "A commitment to social justice." He looked at Rachel when he said it, and he blushed bright red. She smiled at him. It was pretty clear he'd always liked her, but Rachel was used to boys liking her. And there was something different about Carter, anyway. Something kind of special—in a friendly way, not a romantic way. Rachel was no snob, but she'd never go for Carter Bump. She had certain standards of sexiness to adhere to.

"I'm probably saying it wrong," Carter said. "I don't mean to sound offensive."

"You don't sound offensive," Sivan said kindly. Carter was a nice kid. Nobody would call him "cool," but Sivan generally didn't have anything in common with the cool kids (primary example: the cuntriad of Peighton, Kaylee, and Brooklynn). "What do you mean?"

Carter hesitated, and then spoke in a rush. "I mean, like, whenever Ms. Deats teaches us about civil rights movements and things like that, it seems like there's this Jewish presence. Like Jewish people are involved.

Remember when she showed us video of that protest in New York in Harlem and those rabbis marched and they got arrested? I mean that's just one example, so, I'm probably wrong."

"Wow, Carter," Rachel said sweetly. "I think that's the most I've ever heard you speak at once." She patted him on the back like you might a little kid.

"Sorry," Carter said. He blushed harder.

"Don't be sorry," Sivan said. "You're not wrong. American Jews have actually been an integral part of social justice movements in the United States for centuries. For example . . ." Sivan launched into an explanation that wouldn't have been out of place during one of her mother's Jewish studies lectures at Rutgers. Gertie watched her with admiration, just as she always did whenever Sivan spoke at length on a topic. Gertie got nervous before school presentations, but not Sivan. Sivan was a natural. She knew facts and figures, but she also knew how to talk to people so they didn't feel like idiots, even though she might obviously have superior knowledge of the subject. Gertie and Rachel always told Sivan that she would make a great teacher, and Sivan said that even though she fully intended to study political science at Harvard and become a community organizer, she could probably see herself getting a teaching certificate too. But only for high school teaching. She wanted mature students. Middle school kids were a nightmare.

Gertie noticed something as Sivan talked to Carter. It was something shitty, and naturally, it involved the cuntriad. Brooklynn, Peighton, and Kaylee stood behind Sivan. Peighton was doing that thing with her hand where you mimic someone talking on and on and on. Brooklynn squatted down, pretending to be Carter, and nodded vigorously. Kaylee snickered and snorted with laughter. Gertie sent them a death stare of her own, which wasn't something she usually (or ever) did. Kaylee noticed, and scowled at her. Then Sivan looked to see what Gertie was looking at, and so did Carter, and Gertie felt super bad because you could just see Carter deflate and Sivan withdraw into herself.

"Anyway," Sivan said lamely. "That's all I had to say."

"No, you had more," Rachel said, glaring at the cuntriad. "Keep going. It was interesting. And Carter probably had more questions, right?"

"It's okay," Carter said quietly.

"We can talk later," Sivan said. "Look, there's the tour guide."

The cuntriad smiled as one unit, and Gertie thought to herself that she'd never met a shittier trio of human beings.

The sophomore class obediently flocked to Mr. Kenner and Ms. Deats when signaled. Their tour guide, a pretty young woman, introduced herself as Rhonda and said that she'd recently graduated from Rutgers so she was especially excited to lead a tour of kids from New Jersey.

"What was your major?" Ms. Deats asked brightly.

"Jewish studies," Rhonda said.

"Oh my God, I bet you had Sivan's mom!" Rachel said. "Did you know Babs Finkelstein?"

Rhonda's face lit up. "She was my adviser!" she said excitedly. "I love Babs. And you're Sivan! Oh, I've heard so much about you."

Still shaken from being mocked by the cuntriad for what felt like the umpteenth time that week, Sivan could only muster a weak smile. She rubbed the back of her head and wished Rachel hadn't felt the need to bring it up.

"You probably know, like, everything we're going to learn today," Rhonda said to Sivan. "Your granddad was on the planning committee for the museum, right?"

"Yeah," Sivan said. "Yeah, he was."

"Oh, Sivan knows *everything* Jewish," Brooklynn said loudly. "She's like, an expert Jewish person. Just ask her." Rachel stared at her archnemesis. Kaylee and Peighton tittered, and Mr. Kenner gave them a piercing look. They shut up immediately. Rachel's gaze didn't waver.

"What are *you* looking at?" Brooklynn hissed.

Rachel just smiled and turned away. If you didn't know her, you'd think it was just an innocent smile. But Gertie could tell Rachel was *pissed*. If there was one thing Rachel hated, it was a bully. Rachel had always stood up for the kids who got picked on, and it made her furious to see her best friends the victims of insults.

Rhonda explained the rules of the museum: no flash photography; no video or audio recording permitted; no loud voices; no cell phone use inside the museum.

"Well *that* won't be an issue," Brooklynn said resentfully, too quietly for any of the adults to hear.

The students followed Rhonda quietly as they entered the first exhibit, which defined genocide in general and the Holocaust in particular. There were photographs and a few video installations and many artifacts, like precious things the Nazis had stolen from synagogues, plus examples of the yellow stars Jews wore to mark their lower status. Gertie found it all fascinating and deeply sad, and she was actually surprised to see how her classmates behaved. Ever the worrywart, Gertie had been concerned that some of the kids would act like assholes. But even the rowdy kids, like Brock Chuddford, got quiet and somber as they moved through the museum, especially when they came upon photographs of teens and little kids who'd been forced into the camps.

At one point, Gertie heard sniffling behind her. She turned and saw Kaylee wipe away tears while Brooklynn put her arm around the cheerleader.

"I thought I was sad when they took away our cell phones," Kaylee whispered. "But this is like, way worse. I hate this trip."

"It'll get better," Brooklynn cooed sympathetically. "Maybe there's a pool at our hotel."

"There better be." Kaylee pouted. "I am like seriously depressed right now."

They watched a video with survivor stories, and a short film about Anne Frank. There were interactive exhibits and sobering moments, like when they came upon a pile of shoes that had been discarded when victims were sent to the gas chambers. Gertie couldn't believe the shoes were just there, close enough to touch (though of course she would never touch them).

"I always heard about this stuff in school," Rachel said to Sivan and Gertie in a low voice. "Like remember in fifth grade when we read *Number the Stars*? But this place makes it feel real. I think this is the most important museum I've ever visited." Gertie nodded her agreement.

"I've been here a bunch," Sivan said. "But every time I come, I see something new."

Rhonda told them they were almost at the end of their journey, where they could go into the museum shop. But first, they watched another short film, this one about a Lithuanian survivor who had been a little boy in one of the concentration camps and had grown up to be a professor and historian who helped Jewish families trace their roots. Photos of him as a nine-year-old boy flashed onscreen. And behind Sivan, Gertie, and Rachel, there was a little bit of giggling. It wasn't so loud that the teachers could hear, but it was loud enough that the girls could hear. And then came the next part, which was definitely loud enough for Gertie to hear.

"Oh my God," Brooklynn whispered. "That little boy looks exactly like Sivan." At this, Sivan's back stiffened, though she gave no other indication she'd heard.

"Right?" Kaylee said. "That's totally what I was thinking."

"Two little Jewish boys," Brooklynn snickered.

Sivan's shoulders slumped. Rachel got very still the way she did when she was truly enraged. Gertie whipped her head around, ready to tell the cuntriad to shut the fuck up, when something highly unusual occurred.

"Shh," Peighton said. "Don't say that." Sivan looked confused.

"It's not cool," Peighton said quietly.

"Oh, whatever," Brooklynn said. "It was just a joke. Lighten up."

"It wasn't funny," Peighton said.

"Okay, let's drop it," Brooklynn said, and Peighton said no more. Kaylee stared at both of them with big saucer eyes. It was the first time Gertie had ever heard one of them contradict the other, and it seemed it was Kaylee's first time too.

Sivan sat quietly and wondered again who Peighton really was.

Rachel turned around and flashed that same innocent-looking smile at Brooklynn, just as she'd done in the lobby before they began their tour. Brooklynn sneered at her. Then Rachel turned back around to face the screen. She smoothed her hair. She leaned forward and tapped the shoulder of the person sitting in front of her: Brock Chuddford.

"Hi, Brock," she whispered, laying a hand on his shoulder. He half-turned and looked right into her big, beautiful blue eyes. Brock smiled. Behind her, Rachel could feel Brooklynn's horror. Which is exactly why she grabbed Brock's face and kissed him.

There was a pause while the kids in their area noticed what was going on. They were in the back of the theatre, and the teachers were standing off to the side with Rhonda, so it wasn't super-obvious. Until a few seconds later, when Brooklynn shook off her shock and made it pretty evident that something was going on.

"Wow," Gertie whispered as the kiss went on and on.

"This is the most epic Rachel move of all time," Sivan whispered back.

"Are you *fucking* kidding me?" Brooklynn shrieked, jumping up and lunging for Rachel. Peighton sprang into action once again, holding her back, but Brooklynn still managed to yank Rachel's hair. The students in the front of the theater turned around and stared, and Ms. Deats and Mr. Kenner ran into the crowd to separate the girls. Rhonda looked startled.

"Brooklynn! Rachel!" Mr. Kenner hissed. "Outside. NOW."

"I'm so sorry, Rhonda," Ms. Deats said, totally embarrassed. "We'll take care of this outside. Everyone else, keep watching the film."

"No problem," Rhonda said, hushing the rest of the students.

Kaylee and Peighton followed Brooklynn outside, just as Gertie and Sivan followed Rachel. Mr. Kenner marched into a small corridor with restrooms and water fountains. He whipped around and stared at the other girls.

"What the hell are the rest of you girls doing out here?" Mr. Kenner demanded. "Go inside and sit down."

"Rachel was only standing up for me," Sivan said.

"By doing what?" Peighton snapped. "Being a whore?" Apparently any goodwill or empathy she'd felt toward Sivan for a moment had dissipated.

"Peighton!" Ms. Deats said, aghast. "We do not call names, and we do not shame other young women!"

"And we do *not* yell profanity in the middle of a documentary film at the *Holocaust Museum*!" Mr. Kenner spat, shaking with anger. "Brooklynn, that's your first strike."

"That's not fair!" Kaylee said.

"It's Rachel's fault!" Peighton said.

"I fail to see how it can possibly be Rachel's fault that Brooklyn shouted obscenities and attempted to physically attack her in the middle of a quiet theater," Mr. Kenner said.

"She *provoked* me," Brooklynn protested.

"Brooklynn, it's very important to exercise self-control," Ms. Deats said. "Did Rachel hit you?"

"Of course I didn't!" Rachel said.

"Rachel would never do that," Gertie said.

"Rachel isn't a violent person," Sivan said.

"Oh, shut up, Sivan," Peighton snapped. It was like she was making up for being nice earlier.

Sivan lost her temper then, finally.

"*You* shut up, *Peighton!*" Sivan said loudly. She didn't quite shout it, but a nearby security guard shushed her.

"That's it," Mr. Kenner said. "Everybody gets a first strike. All of you. I don't care how it started, but this is where it ends."

The girls all looked as if they were going to cry. Brooklynn actually started to cry, rather noisily. Ms. Deats handed her a tissue and looked at Mr. Kenner reproachfully.

"Now, now," she said. "Maybe there's some way to make this better."

"And what exactly would you suggest?" Mr. Kenner asked.

"This could be—a teachable moment," Ms. Deats said. "It doesn't have to be a first strike. It can be a chance for these girls to work through some of the tensions that have created this conflict."

Mr. Kenner rolled his eyes and threw up his hands.

"Okay, Alicia," he said. "Whatever you say." He stalked back into the theater. Now Ms. Deats kind of looked like *she* might be about to cry.

The six girls looked at one another wordlessly. They may have been in two very separate groups and they may have hated each other's guts, but they'd just witnessed some kind of weird tension between Ms. Deats and Mr. Kenner, and *that* was pretty noteworthy. Even Brooklynn stopped crying and looked intrigued.

"Jeez, he's pissed," Kaylee said.

"Are you guys having some issues?" Rachel asked sympathetically. "Anything you want to talk about, Ms. Deats?"

"No, Rachel, I do not want to talk about anything," Ms. Deats said testily. "Other than the fact that all of you girls need to agree to get along for the rest of this trip, or else. You are not going to make this trip miserable for everyone else just because of your own petty differences. There are too many women in this world who tear one another down instead of building one another up. We all need to look out for one another, not engage in some misguided battle for supremacy."

"Ooh, like white supremacy?" Kaylee whispered fearfully. Clearly, the exhibit on nationalism and hate had penetrated her lovely, thick skull.

"She doesn't mean white supremacy," Peighton said.

"Okay, good," Kaylee said. "What does she mean then?"

Ms. Deats looked at Peighton and Kaylee in confusion, then decided to drop it.

"All right," Ms. Deats said. "Everyone join hands."

"Oh, no," Brooklynn moaned. "Seriously?"

"You're not really in a position to argue, Brooklynn," Ms. Deats said, with apparent annoyance. Ms. Deats almost never seemed annoyed, so they knew she meant business. Begrudgingly, Peighton joined hands with Gertie, who joined hands with Rachel, who held Kaylee's hand, who gingerly held Sivan's hand, who held Brooklynn's hand. Ms. Deats stood between Brooklyn and Peighton, completing the circle.

"Okay," Ms. Deats said pleasantly. "Let's all take a deep breath as a group. Like I taught you in yoga. Big inhale, really get that air down into your bellies."

"Breathing into my belly makes me feel fat," said Kaylee.

"You need to release your body judgment right now and just go with the flow, Kaylee," Ms. Deats said.

"But I don't have my period," Kaylee said.

"Just do what she says," Brooklynn whispered.

The girls breathed in as a group, and then exhaled as a group.

"Now," Ms. Deats said. "Would anyone like to release any resentment by, say, making an apology?"

"I am not apologizing to anyone," Brooklynn said.

"Me neither," Peighton said, tilting her chin up defiantly.

"I don't even know what I would apologize for," Kaylee said.

"I'll go," Rachel said sweetly. "Brooklynn, I am genuinely sorry you are so hostile toward me. I'd really like to do what I can to make things better between us." Gertie and Sivan looked at each other and tried not to grin.

"That's wonderful, Rachel," Ms. Deats said approvingly. "Brooklynn, what do you say in response? Remember that you don't want to get that first strike."

Brooklynn looked at her friends helplessly. They looked back at her, unable to do anything.

"I'm sorry I got so upset with you, Rachel," Brooklynn finally muttered.

"And?" Ms. Deats prompted her.

"And I'm sorry I tried to hit you," Brooklynn said.

"Thank you, Brooklynn," Rachel said. "That honestly means a lot to me."

"I'm sorry, but I really have to pee," Kaylee blurted out. "Can I go pee and then come back to the circle?"

"I think the circle has accomplished what was necessary," Ms. Deats said, enormously pleased. "Let's all take one more group breath, and then let's put this ugliness behind us." The girls did as she told them. Well, they did the first part, anyway, and all inhaled one deep breath.

After the "unfortunate incident" in the theater, as Ms. Deats called it (Mr. Kenner preferred to term it a "childish tantrum"), Rhonda escorted everyone to the museum shop. They would have a half hour to look around and make some purchases before they were due back on the bus, at which point they'd go to a restaurant for an early dinner and then to their hotel "where you can relax," Ms. Deats said.

"And study," Mr. Kenner said.

"Well yes, of course," Ms. Deats said quickly. "They know that."

"Do they?" Mr. Kenner asked drily, and then walked over to help Carter Bump get a copy of *Night* by Elie Wiesel off a high shelf (it was really on a pretty easy-to-reach shelf for a sixteen year old of normal height, but nothing was easy for Carter Bump to reach). After he handed the book to Carter, he moved on.

From a few feet away, Rachel watched as Carter dug into the book with evident eagerness. Then Brock Chuddford strode up to Carter and clamped a hand on his shoulder.

"Oh shit," Rachel said quietly to herself. She'd only kissed Brock to piss off Brooklynn; he was kind of a doofus and teased people sometimes, although she'd never actually seen him be mean. Still, her bully detector went off, and she prepared to act.

"What's that?" Brock asked suspiciously.

"What's what?"

"That." Brock pointed to *Night*.

"It's just a book," Carter said, hiding it behind his back. "It's nothing."

"Give it to me," Brock ordered him, and Carter obeyed.

Rachel didn't like to see the fear in Carter's eyes, but she was smart enough not to embarrass a guy by stepping in unless it was absolutely necessary. Rachel knew Carter didn't have a dad, because his dad had died in Afghanistan. That was kind of a lot of pressure. And when you're short and nerdy and fat and you don't have any big brothers to stick up for you, it's not like you have an easy time in school, either. Rachel remembered Carter getting beaten up a lot in middle school, although that had seemed to cease once they hit high school.

But Carter Bump had good reason to cringe when Brock Chuddford told him to hand over *Night*. The possibilities were as follows: 1.) Brock would make fun of him for reading a boring-looking book; 2.) Brock would whack him in the head with the book and then laugh loudly; 3.) Brock would call his buddies over and one of *them* would whack Carter in the head with the book; 4.) Mr. Kenner would notice something amiss and come over and break up the situation. Rachel figured her intervention was option number 5.

And then Brock Chuddford did something that surprised Rachel.

He looked at the book with evident interest.

"Is this good?" he asked Carter.

"Are you—are you, like, joking?" Carter asked uncertainly.

"Little dude, I wouldn't joke at the Holocaust Museum," Brock said seriously. "Would you?"

"No," Carter said.

"So is this good or what?" Brock asked again.

"I heard it's really good," Carter said. "It's about a man who survived the Holocaust. He's pretty famous."

"Elie is a dude's name?" Brock said.

"I guess in the country he came from," Carter said. "I think he came from Hungary."

Brock looked at the book curiously.

"You think it's hard to read?" Brock asked.

"I'm sure it's really sad," Carter said.

"Oh, I don't care about that," Brock said. "I'm good with sad. I just mean, like, do you think it's complicated?"

Rachel understood then that what Brock was asking was whether Carter had the confidence that Brock would be capable of understanding the words on the page.

There was something so strangely sweet about this whole interaction.

"Well," Carter said carefully. "A lot of people read it and they seem to like it. So it can't be that hard to understand, because it's really popular, and stuff that's hard to understand is never popular. But it's supposed to be really good."

Brock thought about that for a second. Then he reached out and pulled another copy of *Night* off the shelf.

"I might have questions for you," Brock said. And without another word, he gave Carter's copy back to him and took his own copy to the register.

Carter looked at his own book, then at Brock, then at the book, then at Brock.

Then he looked at Rachel. She looked at him and shook her head in disbelief. Then she grinned.

He grinned back.

Well, that had been . . . unexpected.

Gertie was off in a corner by herself, looking through a beautiful book of photography of Holocaust survivors and their descendants, when she heard a familiar voice.

"I'm fine," it said. "Thanks, Mr. Bauer."

Gertie's head snapped up as if she were a hunting dog who had heard the rustle of something in the underbrush. Slowly, very slowly, she turned her head and laid eyes on a handsome boy who stood not twelve feet away, wiping tears from his eyes and talking to a concerned-looking middle-aged man.

Danny Bryan.

Gertie's face went completely white. She sank into a nearby chair—thank goodness it was there, or else she probably would've just fallen on the floor. Across the shop, Rachel looked up at just that moment and saw Gertie. Rachel hurried over to Sivan.

"It happened again," Rachel whispered to Sivan.

"What happened?" Sivan asked. She was deeply intrigued by a book of translated Yiddish poetry and wanted to focus her energies on that, disappear into the words and get a break from the dumb realities of this D.C. trip for a moment.

"My psychic thing," Rachel said. "I got this weird tingly feeling, and I looked up, and I saw *that*."

"Rachel, you really need to get over *American Horror Story: Coven*," Sivan said. "It's not real life." Then she looked at where Rachel was pointing, and saw Gertie's face.

"Oh no," Sivan said. "She looks sick. Maybe it was the lunch her mom packed her. You know her mom isn't much of a cook." The girls hurried over and knelt down beside Gertie, who appeared nearly catatonic.

"Gertie," Sivan said tentatively. "You okay?"

Gertie murmured something unintelligible. The girls leaned in closer.

"Danny Bryan is right over there," she whispered, pointing. They looked and sure enough, it was the guy they'd seen a million times on Instagram and Facebook and in Gertie's annual camp yearbooks.

"No shit," Rachel said excitedly. "Gertie, go say hi to him."

"No way," Gertie said. Because as soon as she'd seen him, she'd been seized by a powerful feeling that now was not the time to interact with him. He looked like he was having a private moment, and maybe that other guy was a teacher who was trying to guide him through the moment, and Gertie didn't want to ruin the moment, and also she had like this Pavlovian reaction to seeing Danny Bryan that dictated that she had to freak out, like, every single time she saw him.

"I'll talk to him, then," Rachel said lightly, and before she could make a move, Gertie's nails were digging into her arm.

"Fucking ow!" Rachel said, snatching her arm away. "You almost drew blood."

"I don't want to talk to him," Gertie said resolutely. "Not now. This isn't the way it's supposed to happen."

"Gertie," Rachel said. "As someone who is maybe kind of psychic, I feel like this trip is your chance to actually get to talk to Danny Bryan for real, as a grown young woman and not some geeky little girl. And my senses are telling me that if you talk to him, good things will happen, and you really don't have to worry about it. So therefore, I think you should talk to him right now."

"He's been here for a while," Sivan said. "We saw that Instagram a few hours ago. His class must be here too." She indicated a group of older boys and girls milling around the teacher who had been concerned about Danny. One of the kids wore a Lindbergh High School football T-shirt, and Gertie pointed it out in a whisper.

"So let's go talk to them," Rachel said. "C'mon. I won't talk to Danny. I'll just gather some information." She stood up and brushed herself off.

"Rachel, Gertie doesn't want you to," Sivan said.

"But I want me to," Rachel said.

You couldn't argue with that kind of logic. And so despite Gertie's obvious feeling of wanting to curl up in a ball and die, Rachel confidently stepped off in the direction where the Lindbergh High School kids were gathered.

"Wow, you guys go to Lindbergh?" she said to the kid in the Lindbergh T-shirt.

"Yeah," he said. "In Jersey."

"We're from Flemington," she said.

"Oh, for real?" he said. "No shit. That's cool."

"Yeah," she said. "We're staying at some Holiday Inn somewhere. Is that where you guys are staying?"

"No," he said. "We're—hey, Danny, what's our hotel called again?"

Danny Bryan turned and looked at Rachel and the other guy. From twelve feet away, Gertie's entire being clenched in anxiety.

"We're at the Henry Hotel," he said. "Bro, we've been there a day and you can't remember?"

The kid laughed, and Rachel smiled prettily.

"Have a great trip!" Rachel said.

"Thanks," said the kid, looking her up and down.

Rachel was already walking away, triumphant.

"What happened?" Gertie whispered.

"They're staying at the Henry Hotel," Rachel said. "And you're welcome, Gertrude."

"You didn't mention me, did you?" Gertie said fretfully.

"Of course not," Rachel said. "I respected your wishes. Anyway, how are we going to get to the Henry Hotel?"

"We're not," Sivan said. "That's ridiculous. They're already pissed at us. Do you want to get us expelled?"

"We won't get expelled," Rachel said smoothly. "Trust me."

"The last time I trusted you with something this important, I got a tampon stuck inside me," Gertie said, shivering at the memory.

Rachel sighed. "Gertie, you did not get a tampon stuck inside you. I told you how to put it in, and you did and it was totally fine, and then you immediately got super-nervous and tried to yank it out, and your pussy muscles clenched and I had to talk you down with deep-breathing exercises. I should've gotten you high before you tried it."

"Please don't talk about pussy muscles here," Sivan said, gesturing to their surroundings.

"I'm sorry," Rachel said. "I feel like I always end up saying the wrong thing with you. I feel like a really offensive person."

"Do you really feel that way?" Sivan asked, genuinely touched.

Rachel giggled.

"Nah," she said. "You're just kind of uptight. But I love you for it." She hugged Sivan, who rolled her eyes.

"Look," Gertie said. "They're leaving." It was true. All the kids from Lindbergh were filing out of the museum shop after their teacher.

"Last chance to say something to him, Gertie," Sivan said. Gertie looked at her, surprised.

"I'm not trying to pressure you or anything," Sivan added quickly. "I just don't want you to be disappointed again like you are when you come home every summer."

"Oh, it's not her last chance to say something to him," Rachel said confidently.

"Let me guess," Sivan said. "Your psychic powers have told you we'll see him again."

"Exactly," Rachel said.

And just like that, Danny Bryan and his companions were gone.

Against her better judgment, Alicia Deats went up to
Brian Kenner in the documentaries section of the museum
shop. He was looking at a DVD about Leni Riefenstahl,
and didn't see her come up.

She cleared her throat. He jumped a little, and looked
annoyed when he saw who it was.

"You like documentaries?" she said awkwardly. The
kids were all occupied with one thing or another, and she
figured she may as well open with something neutral in
order to smooth over their earlier differences.

"On Netflix, yes," Brian said, putting the documentary
away. "I've seen this one. I was just interested in how they
market it in the hard copy as opposed to online."

"Oh," Alicia said. "Yes. I don't have Netflix. I actually
don't have a TV."

He nodded and looked at the ground. They stood in
awkward silence for a long moment.

"I used to have one," she said. "I used to love TV. I
watched a lot of BBC America and Syfy stuff."

Brian looked mildly surprised. "Me too," he said. "Why'd you stop?"

"It's a long story," Alicia said, because it was. She looked at her feet for a moment and studied her toes. Her mother and her sister, the Republican corporate lawyer, always said she ought to at least get a manicure if she was going to insist on wearing those hippie Birkenstocks all the time, but Alicia couldn't think of anything sillier than a girl in Birkenstocks walking around in pink toenail polish or something like that. She liked Birkenstocks because they were low-maintenance, and comfortable, and getting pedicures made her feel sad for the poorly paid women who had to scrub stuff off people's feet all day. She wasn't really the pedicure kind of gal.

She looked up, and Brian was gone.

Just gone. He'd walked away, right in the middle of what was shaping up to be kind of a decent conversation, maybe.

Great. Fucking great.

How many hours til they got home? Forty-five?

She was already counting down.

"Well," said **Mr. Kenner** in his booming announcement voice that echoed through the bus. "Despite the antics of a few of the girls during the final film, I'd say the trip to the Holocaust Museum was almost a success." They were all packed onto the bus, which was rolling along the streets of D.C. at a pretty decent pace, considering it was just about the beginning of rush hour.

"It's time for dinner," he continued. "There happens to be a restaurant right across the parking lot from our hotel, so we'll eat there tonight."

"What restaurant is it?" Kaylee asked. "I'm a vegetarian."

"Weren't you eating beef jerky in my classroom two days ago?" Mr. Kenner asked.

"Yeah, but I read a thing that says meat makes you break out," Kaylee said. "And there's a dance next month."

Mr. Kenner paused. Kaylee looked at him.

"And?" he said.

"And what?" she asked.

"And that's the only reason you're a vegetarian for the next four weeks? The end-of-year dance?"

"Well, yeah," Kaylee said. "I mean, what other reason do I need?"

"Well I applaud your commitment to a kinder diet, Kaylee," Ms. Deats said, ignoring Mr. Kenner. "If you stick with it, you'll reap the rewards for years to come."

Kaylee looked at Brooklynn, confused.

"B," Kaylee said. "Did she just say I'll r—"

"No, honey," Brooklynn said. "She didn't say you'll rape anything."

"Because it really sounded like she said that," Kaylee said.

"It did sound a little bit like that," Peighton said. "But that's not what she meant."

"Okay, good," Kaylee said. "Because I'm not the type of person who would rape anything. Or anybody."

"Of course you aren't," Brooklynn said.

From a few seats away, Sivan barely stifled a groan.

"She can't seriously be that stupid," Gertie said.

"Oh, she is," Rachel said. "And it's glorious. Like I know I'm not good in anything but English class, but every time Kaylee opens her mouth in class I just feel like a genius."

"So where exactly are we going to dinner?" Kaylee asked.

Mr. Kenner looked over his glasses at her.

"OMG Thursdays," he said.

A massive squeal of joy rose up from the students. Ms. Deats smiled. Sixteen-year-olds were practically adults, but they still acted like little kids sometimes. This was definitely one of those times. Olivia was practically jumping up and down in her seat. Carter Bump looked as if he'd just won the lottery. Even Brooklynn, Peighton, and Kaylee, who usually turned up their noses at things, looked absolutely delighted. Kaitlynne and Olivia hugged.

OMG Thursdays was perhaps the most popular chain restaurant franchise in Flemington, New Jersey. It had only opened a branch in Flemington the previous summer, and no one in town was yet accustomed to the excitement of having a huge, colorful, noisy OMG Thursdays so conveniently close to other major Flemington attractions, like the outlet mall and the highway exit. It was really quite thrilling to go to OMG Thursdays and eat an O-M-Gigantic Steak™ basted in special Malibu Rum Secret Sauce™ and wash it down with an O-M-Ginormous Watermelon Margarita Blaster™ (virgin for the kids, of course), always available with a complimentary side of Sexy MexiCaliTexan Nachitos Buenos™. The fried Snickers Popcorn Balls™ were also amazing— popcorn coated in melted Snickers bars, rolled into a ball, dipped in beer batter, and deep-fried to perfection. OMG Thursdays had a twenty-page menu, of which five full pages were devoted to desserts. It was perfect.

Sivan was no fan of OMG Thursdays, given that her father and a board of community activists had tried to fight the demolition of the landmark 1937 diner that had previously occupied its lot. Rachel had never actually been to an OMG Thursdays, as her parents frowned on entering any establishment with a liquor license. And Gertie always got a weird headache from the glaringly bright lights, flashing disco balls, blaring jukebox, and general hectic atmosphere. But they were perhaps the only three people on the bus who displayed no amount of excitement over OMG Thursdays. Despite her loyalty to the cause of historic preservation, Sivan had always had a sneaking desire to try the famed Green Bean-a-rinos™, which were vegan fried green beans that allegedly tasted absolutely amazing, according to Ms. Bump, the gym teacher. Ms. Bump wasn't even a vegan, but she got those fried green beans every single time she went to OMG Thursdays with the other gym teachers, and she always raved about them in gym class the next day.

The bus pulled into the parking lot, and there was the Holiday Inn, OMG Thursdays, and a freestanding Rite Aid pharmacy.

Rachel had an idea. She was always full of great ideas, but this one was particularly good. When the bus came to a halt, she waited her turn to file off the bus. But before she did, she leaned over and whispered a question to Ms. Deats, who immediately gave a sympathetic nod of assent.

And as Mr. Kenner did the head count in the parking lot, Rachel scurried over to the Rite Aid and disappeared inside.

"What is Rachel doing at the Rite Aid?" Mr. Kenner asked Ms. Deats. "Did you approve that?"

"I did," Ms. Deats said.

"Without a chaperone?" he demanded. The students quieted to listen in on what seemed like a brewing fight.

"I—well, yes," Ms. Deats said. She was clearly embarrassed.

"Why?" Mr. Kenner said. "You know that's against protocol."

Ms. Deats leaned over and whispered in his ear, and his expression changed.

"Oh," he said, turning red. "That's fine, then. All right."

"Tampon run!" Brooklynn sang out, and a bunch of the kids laughed. Sivan and Gertie glared at her, but she ignored them. She was having too much fun.

"Enough, Brooklynn," Ms. Deats said. "Remember the circle of forgiveness."

"I'm sorry," Brooklynn said contritely. As soon as Ms. Deats turned her back, Brooklynn lowered her voice and said, "At least we know Rachel isn't pregnant."

"Yet," Peighton said, and the two girls snickered.

"Wait, how do we know that?" Kaylee asked.

"Because she has her period, honey," Brooklynn said with a sigh.

"Ohhhhh," Kaylee said. "Oh, *that's* why she had to go to the pharmacy."

"Yeah, probably to buy like extra-huge tampons," Peighton said.

Kaylee looked confused again.

"Because of all the dicks she's had inside her, sweetie," Brooklynn explained patiently.

"Oh!" Kaylee started laughing. "Oh, gross!"

"I fucking *hate* those cunts," Gertie whispered to Sivan, her fists clenched.

"Me too," Sivan said. "Although maybe we don't have to use a gendered term anymore. We could just call them assholes. Everybody has those."

"And there's nothing we can do about them," Gertie barreled on. "That's the shittiest thing. They're just always going to be there. You know Kaylee will check out my phone when I'm listening to music in study hall, and whatever track she sees on the screen, she'll tell me it sucks? Like do you think Kaylee has even *heard* of Sleater-Kinney or Le Tigre?"

"I mean, I haven't either," Sivan said. "But I just listen to hip-hop."

"You and your dad," Gertie said fondly. Noah Finkelstein was always listening to Mos Def or Talib Kweli or Dead Prez outside while he did yard work at the Finkelsteins' house. She and Sivan had tried to explain to him that he could just listen on headphones, but he preferred to hook up his ancient iPod to speakers and just blast, like,

N.W.A. at 8 a.m. on a Sunday. His neighbors (the Chuddfords) did *not* know what to do.

Rachel returned from the Rite Aid, carrying a bag and looking embarrassed. This was rare for Rachel.

"Sorry to make everybody wait, Mr. Kenner," she said with uncharacteristic shyness.

"That's fine, Rachel," Mr. Kenner said. "Health comes first."

She re-entered the pack of students, ignoring the smirks from the cuntriad.

The class filed into OMG Thursdays. Because it was early in the dinner shift (and, of course, because Mr. Kenner had called ahead), they were seated in an empty section of the enormous dining room.

Peighton, Kaylee, and Brooklynn staked their claim on three seats at the end of a long table. To their surprise (and Gertie's and Sivan's), Rachel made a beeline for them.

"I'm so glad we made up," Rachel said smoothly, sliding into the seat right beside Brooklynn. "Now we can enjoy dinner together. I'm sorry about earlier. I don't know what happened to me. I get so carried away sometimes. I think it's like a real problem."

Gertie and Sivan looked at each other, confused.

"C'mon, girls!" Rachel said, beckoning them. "Sivan, you sit next to Kaylee and Peighton. Gertie, you come sit next to me and Brooklynn."

Brooklynn opened her mouth to protest, but suddenly Ms. Deats was upon them, looking absolutely delighted.

"Girls, I have to tell you, this is really inspiring," she said, her eyes shining. She patted Brooklynn and Rachel on the back. "The way you're reaching out and making an effort to work together is just so fantastic. If I could give you the opposite of a strike, I would! I'm just so pleased."

Brooklynn closed her mouth into a thin, straight line.

"Well, it's all because of you," Rachel said. "You made the difference."

Ms. Deats blushed.

"Oh, stop," she said. "That is just too kind." Then she moved along and found her own seat in the middle of the table.

Mr. Kenner explained the rules: they could each order a soda or iced tea ("Nothing from the bar, even without alcohol!" he said sternly, looking at Olivia, who looked visibly disappointed) and an entrée.

"What about dessert?" Olivia asked desperately.

"No dessert," Mr. Kenner said. "We're on the school's credit card here."

A whine of protest rose up from the assembled students.

"Processed sugar is a killer," Ms. Deats said. "It saps your strength and causes terrible diseases."

The students only whined louder.

"Well, I'm sure there will be vending machines in the hotel," she said. "If you *must* have dessert. But nobody is allowed to order room service."

"What about late-night pizza?" Brock Chuddford asked. A couple of his lacrosse buddies burst out laughing and high-fived him. They burst out laughing and high-fived him every time he said anything. He was their boy king.

"Absolutely not," Mr. Kenner said. "We'll go over the rules for tonight later. But they are strict. And if you break them, you will be punished."

"I was just kidding, bro," Brock mumbled.

"What's that, Brock?" Mr. Kenner asked. "I couldn't quite hear you."

"Nothing," Brock said. "Sorry I asked."

"Remember that you already have one strike," Mr. Kenner said. "You wouldn't be alone in that distinction if I had my choice." He glared at the girls seated at the end of the table, and they all looked back at him innocently. Rachel wasn't the only one who knew how to fake it.

The meal got under way, and Brooklynn, Peighton, and Kaylee made a big show of ignoring Rachel, Sivan, and Gertie. The cuntriad chattered among themselves, mostly about the big dance. They all ordered iced tea from the bored-looking waitress.

"I'll have an iced tea too," Rachel said brightly. "If you want, you can just bring us a pitcher. If that's easier."

"I guess," the waitress said listlessly.

"I'll have—" Gertie began, and Rachel cut her off.

"She'll have a Coke," Rachel said. "And Sivan over there will have the same."

"But I wanted iced tea too," Gertie said.

"No, you didn't," Rachel said, poking Gertie under the table. "Iced tea is for people who are watching their weight. You don't have to worry about that."

Kaylee snickered and mumbled something to Peighton, who started giggling too. Gertie stared at Sivan, and Sivan stared back, because they both wanted to hit these jerks. And also, what was Rachel doing?

The drinks arrived, and Rachel tried to pour iced tea for everyone who'd ordered it.

"I can pour my own," Brooklynn said, snatching the pitcher away. Rachel looked irritated for a moment, and then the usual carefree smile appeared on her face.

"No worries," she said.

"What does that even mean?" Peighton snapped. "No worries. Dumb. There's always something to worry about."

"That's true," Rachel agreed. "I'll have to stop saying it." Peighton gave her a hard look, but there was no trace of sarcasm in Rachel's voice, no evidence of insincerity in her face.

"Well . . . whatever," Peighton said, shrugging.

When the entrees were served, Brooklynn looked at Peighton and Kaylee.

"I have to pee," she announced.

"Okay," Kaylee said, with a mouthful of grilled chicken. Brooklynn looked at her expectantly.

"She means we should go with her," Peighton said. "We always go together."

"Oh, right," Kaylee said, swallowing her chicken. "I know. I'm just really loving this chicken."

"You know, Gertie and Sivan have to go too," Rachel said.

"No, I definitely—" Sivan said, but Rachel jumped back in.

"I know how tiny your bladders are," Rachel said, poking Gertie again under the table. Gertie didn't know exactly what the point of this exercise was, but she knew she was supposed to go to the bathroom. Whatever Rachel was up to, they'd probably find out soon enough.

"Yeah, c'mon, Sivan," Gertie said. "Let's go with them."

Peighton, Brooklynn, and Kaylee looked annoyed and marched off as quickly as they could. Gertie and Sivan followed at a distance.

"What is Rachel doing?" Sivan asked Gertie in a low voice.

"I have no idea," Gertie replied. "She kept poking me under the table."

When they reached the bathroom, Peighton was primping in front of a mirror. She turned and looked at Sivan.

"Shouldn't you be in the men's room?" she asked. Kaylee and Brooklynn were already in stalls, and they cackled.

"Peighton, you bitch," Brooklynn said admiringly.

Sivan and Gertie went into stalls. Sivan just sat there for a few minutes, trying hard not to feel like she was some kind of bug Peighton could squash for her own pleasure. Gertie found that she actually did have to pee. Maybe it was the sound of running water while the other girls washed their hands, but it inspired her.

Gertie and Sivan emerged from the stalls at the same time, and found Brooklynn, Peighton, and Kaylee staring at them. For a moment, Gertie wondered if the girls were going to try to beat them up or something.

"Can we help you?" Sivan asked frostily. She tried to get to the sink, but the girls blocked her.

"You think you're some kind of genius," Peighton said. "But you're not. You're just gross."

"And your friend Rachel is a stupid whore," Brooklynn said.

"Yeah," Kaylee said. "I mean, to both of those things, yes. Yeah."

Sivan tried to keep in mind all the principles of non-violence that her mother and her father and her favorite twentieth-century historical figures had instilled in her. She breathed deeply. The bathroom smelled like stale pee and Lysol. She heard a voice speak up then, and to her surprise, it belonged to Gertie.

"Just get out of our way," Gertie said in a low, steady voice. "Get the fuck out of our way." She pushed past them and stormily began washing her hands.

The girls looked a little surprised at that one.

"Whatever," Brooklynn said. "Let's get out of here."

The cuntriad walked away, but not before Kaylee whispered, "I didn't know Asians *swore*."

"Honey, don't think too hard about it," Brooklynn said, as they walked out the door.

Sivan was silent for a moment after the girls left.

"What was that about?" she asked, joining Gertie at the sink.

Gertie frowned.

"I'll never get to see Danny Bryan again," she said. "I wasn't thinking about it before, but I just realized there's no way I can be a camp counselor this summer. I have to get a full-time real job that pays better so I can contribute to my parents' college fund. We always agreed that once I was sixteen I would get a job and start saving up. So now it's too late to tell him how I feel."

"Oh, Gertie," Sivan sighed.

They both dried their hands and went back to the table. Rachel was nodding vigorously at something Brooklynn was saying.

"I don't get it," Kaylee said as the girls settled down.

"Brooklynn just called you a slut to your face. Why aren't you mad?"

"Oh, I totally agree," Rachel said pleasantly. "It's something I'm working on with a therapist. It's like a real mental issue I have. And I appreciate you reflecting my behavior back to me, Brooklynn."

"She's not a slut," Gertie said.

"No, I definitely am," Rachel said. "It's okay. I'm beginning to figure some things out about myself."

Brooklynn looked at her suspiciously, and then seemed to relent a little.

"Well . . . good," she said. "You should. Because you can't just go around being a slut. It's not cool."

"Totally isn't," Rachel said. "You're right. Hey, where'd you get that necklace?"

Brooklynn was wearing a nameplate necklace.

"My father bought it for me," she said haughtily. "He had it specially made by a jeweler on one of his business trips."

"I wish I had a necklace like that," Rachel said. "It's so pretty."

"You could probably get a 'Rachel' necklace really easy," Brooklynn said. "I mean, it's like a boring name that everybody has."

"Your name is so pretty," Rachel said.

"I know," Brooklynn said. "I was supposed to have a twin and we were going to be Brooke and Lynn, but then she like died in the womb in the first trimester because I was taking up all the nourishment or whatever. That's what the doctor told my mother." Brooklynn looked pleased by this information.

"Wow," Rachel said. "That's amazing."

"I know, right?" Brooklynn said. "I would've gotten so much less attention with a sister." She shivered at the thought.

Finally, after what seemed like forever (though it was only another forty minutes), everyone finished their meals. Mr. Kenner told Ms. Deats that he would pay for the meal on the school credit card if she would take everyone outside and do a head count, and she said she'd really prefer to pay and let him do the head count since he was *so very good at math*, and he said actually she was better suited to working with the crowd of kids since she was so concerned about the "whole child," and that maybe she could manage to count all the whole children, and it was this kind of passive-aggressive thing that reminded more than a few of the students of dinnertime arguments back home.

"Ugh, I just wish they would shut *up*," Brooklynn said as they went on and on. Then she got a funny look on her face.

"Excuse me," she said hurriedly, and got up and rushed away. Peighton and Kaylee looked at each other, utterly shocked that Brooklynn had gone off without them. Then, as if right on schedule, they each blanched and pushed back from the table, walking away at a fast clip.

At just that moment, Ms. Deats and Mr. Kenner settled their dumb fight, or whatever it was. Ms. Deats called for everybody to file out into the parking lot "in a peaceful and orderly fashion," and for the most part, they obeyed (though Brock Chuddford kept trying to give one of his buddies a wedgie). Then she did a quick head count.

"We're three short," she said. "Who's missing?"

"Brooklynn, Peighton, and Kaylee aren't here, Ms. Deats," Rachel said, her sweet voice accentuated by just a little bit of concern. "Would you like for us to look for them?"

"Sure, Rachel," Ms. Deats said. "But don't you three go missing. Come back right away, even if you don't find them."

"We will," Rachel said, and grabbed her two friends, dragging them along.

"What exactly are we doing?" Gertie asked.

"You'll see," Rachel said with that smile of hers.

She led her two friends through the restaurant to the bathroom door. Before she entered, she put her ear to the door and listened. A great look of satisfaction spread across her face.

"You're welcome," she said to Sivan and Gertie, and pushed open the door.

"For what?" Gertie asked, and then nearly gagged at the smell emanating from three of the stalls. The sounds were nearly as bad. Rachel let the door swing shut behind them, and smiled happily.

The cuntriad was experiencing what might best be

described as an explosion of the ass. An "assplosion," if you will.

In between farts and bouts of—well, you know—the girls were freaking out.

"It's like I'm pissing out my butt!" Kaylee practically shrieked.

"What the *fuck* was in my Super Skinny Diet Pizza Nachos?" Brooklynn wailed.

"Oh my God, I've never shit this much in my life," Peighton moaned.

Sivan and Gertie looked at Rachel with wide eyes. Wordlessly, she nodded.

"Shit," Sivan whispered.

"Exactly," Rachel said.

"Who's there?" Brooklynn yelped. "Ms. Deats?"

"Not exactly, sweetie," Rachel said. "How's it going in there?"

"Rachel?" Brooklynn said.

"Yup. Just slutty old me, sluttin' it up over here." Rachel stepped closer to Brooklynn's stall. "You having fun?"

Brooklynn was silent for a solid minute, except for heinous farts.

"It was you!" she finally spat, infuriated. "You did this!"

"C'mon, B," Peighton said. "She's just being a bitch. She couldn't make us sick."

"Don't fucking contradict me, Peighton!" Brooklynn shouted. "You don't fucking know what she's capable of!"

"We'll just let Ms. Deats know you've got a huge case of the shits," Rachel said pleasantly, as if discussing the weather. "We'll make sure everybody knows. You come out whenever you're done. It might be awhile. So sorry this happened to you girls. Really a shame."

"Fuck you!" Brooklynn screamed right before Kaylee let out an enormous fart.

Rachel glided out of the bathroom, pulling Sivan and Gertie along with her.

"Rachel," Sivan whispered. "What did you do?"

"Nothing," Rachel said. "Just picked up a few necessary items at Rite Aid. No big deal."

"I'm like, horrified," Gertie said. "But also impressed. Improrrified?"

"You're amazing, Rachel," Sivan said admiringly. "What made you do that?"

Rachel looked at Sivan as if the answer were obvious.

"They were mean to you," she said. "And to Gertie too. I just got sick of it." She paused and grinned. "And now I guess they're sick of it too."

She linked arms with her two best friends and walked out of the restaurant. Their heads were high, their backs were straight, and all three of them had the feeling this trip was finally starting to get good.

An hour later, the sophomores of Flemington High School settled into their hotel rooms. The students were grouped in threes in rooms with double beds. Much grumbling was done regarding which person in each group of three would have the unlucky job of sharing a bed on both nights of the trip. Gertie, Sivan, and Rachel were fine with it; they'd just flip a coin or something to figure it out, and they'd shared beds plenty of times, so it didn't matter. Peighton, Brooklynn, and Kaylee were too busy taking turns in their hotel bathroom to consider the sleeping situation, although out of pity for them Ms. Deats obtained an extra cot so that each girl could have her own bed that night.

None of the cuntriad squealed on Rachel. They couldn't prove it, for one thing, and they would've sounded totally bonkers if they'd tried to pin their diarrhea on a girl who'd been so publicly sweet to them in the forgiveness circle and at dinner. But they vowed revenge, of course.

Ms. Deats brought the cuntriad Gatorade and Saltine crackers and mint tea, all of which she obtained at the Rite Aid. She offered to sit with them in their room and do reiki on them or at least lead them in a wellness meditation, but they vetoed the idea with such fervor that she left them alone, with instructions to call her immediately via the room phone if the situation didn't improve.

Over in the room where Gertie, Sivan, and Rachel were staying, a shitstorm of another sort was brewing.

"No," Gertie said resolutely, folding her arms. "Absolutely not."

"We're doing it," Rachel said, her eyes glittering the way they did whenever she was psyched about a plan.

"We are NOT doing that!" Gertie declared. She actually stamped her foot, which Rachel thought was kind of adorable.

"Yes, we are," Rachel said simply. She looked in the mirror and pursed her lips, applying some sexy red lipstick she'd picked up at Rite Aid along with the laxatives and a few other key items. She would've been grounded for a week back home if her parents had spotted her with that lipstick.

"Sivan, tell her," Gertie said. "Tell her no."

Sivan looked at Gertie and shrugged.

"I dunno," Sivan said. "I know I wasn't into it earlier, but when I saw the look on your face when you saw him at the museum . . . honestly, I know it's a risk, but it sounds like kind of a cool idea."

"Of course it does!" Rachel crowed triumphantly. "It's an AWESOME idea. Who goes on a trip to D.C. and *doesn't* sneak out?"

"Like, normal people!" Gertie said. "Normal people who don't want to get expelled from school."

"I doubt they'd expel us," Sivan said thoughtfully. "They'd probably suspend us and make us undergo some kind of counseling. Or maybe we'd do community service."

"We already have one strike," Gertie said. "Sneaking out is worth at least two more strikes. At least. We'd have to go to summer school. It would go on our permanent record. You heard them!"

"It's pointless to even think about that, because we're not going to get caught," Rachel said confidently. "It's easy. Ten o'clock is lights out for students. We wait till eleven, after Ms. Deats and Mr. Kenner are asleep. Then we go downstairs and go, well, wherever we want to go! Like, you know, the Henry Hotel." She wiggled her eyebrows suggestively at Gertie.

"No way!" Gertie said resolutely. "We're not going to the Henry Hotel. We don't even know where it is. We don't even know where we are. And I should just give up on loving Danny Bryan because I'm never going to see him again anyway so what's even the point of trying to see him in Washington, D.C.?"

"Okay, so forget Danny Bryan!" Rachel said. "Let's go somewhere else. Let's go to, I don't know, a club or something. It doesn't even matter, to be honest. We just have to do it."

"Why?" Gertie asked. "Why can't we just stay here and go to sleep and wake up and deal with whatever those awful bitches do to us tomorrow, and just get through this trip?"

"Oh, they won't do anything to us tomorrow," Rachel said. "We've defeated them!"

"*You* defeated them temporarily," Gertie said. "And they'll retaliate. I just have a bad feeling about it."

"Would you rather I *hadn't* given them explosive diarrhea?" Rachel demanded, slightly insulted.

The room was quiet for a moment. Then Gertie started cracking up despite herself. Then Rachel did, too, and so did Sivan.

"Oh my God," Sivan said. "That's the best sentence any of us has ever said."

"Goes in the quote book for sure," Gertie said. Back home, they had a quote book (really just a mottled black-and-white Mead notebook) where they wrote down all the best things any one of them ever said. Occasionally at sleepovers they took it out and read stuff from way back in fourth or fifth grade, cracking themselves up at the memories.

"Imagine how many more quotes we'll have for the book after we sneak out tonight," Rachel said.

"I don't know. . . ." Gertie said. "It just doesn't feel like a good idea."

"I think it feels like a great idea," Rachel said. "And I'm probably somewhat psychic, so we should go with my gut. Also, I sneak away from Jesus camp constantly. It's how I got fingered for the first time. You remember the story."

"How could we forget," Sivan said dryly. "You're probably the only girl in history to get fingered by a pastor's kid in an actual graveyard next to a church camp."

"You'd be surprised," Rachel said. "Christians are horny as fuuuuck. And it wasn't something that could make a baby, so it doesn't count."

"Are we really going to have this debate again?" Sivan sighed.

"No, I just mean fingering doesn't count in the world of my ignorant-ass church," Rachel said. "I don't mean it doesn't count in real life. I know it's an important part of lesbian sex because I read about it in *Our Bodies, Ourselves*."

"Can we not talk about fingering, please?" Gertie said. "It makes me think about Danny Bryan, and that just makes me mad."

"I mean, we were technically talking about lesbian fingering," Rachel said.

"Not that fingers have gender," Sivan said.

"Can I ever say anything right around you?" Rachel exclaimed. She was only half joking. Sivan put an arm around her and laid her head on her shoulder.

"I'm just fucking with you," Sivan said. "You're fine."

"Well, we're sneaking out," Rachel said. "That's it. Because we have to live, and do things, and have adventures, and this is an amazing opportunity. Don't you want to have stories to tell our grandkids?"

"Oh, what, like getting fingered in a graveyard?" Gertie said.

"What, you'd rather tell them about how you went to bed on time every night and got up at the right time every morning and went on a school trip to D.C. where you behaved perfectly and never broke any rules?" Rachel said.

Gertie thought for a moment. When Rachel put it that way, Gertie sounded pretty damn boring. Not that she didn't already know that. But maybe Rachel was right. Maybe tonight was an amazing opportunity to do stuff. Gertie wasn't even sure what the stuff would be, but she knew it could be big stuff. Stuff you remembered. Stuff you told stories about years later, but only to your friends, because you wouldn't want your kids or grandkids to know you'd acted like a total delinquent in our nation's capital.

"I think she's coming around," Sivan said with a grin.

"Fine," Gertie relented, and Rachel jumped up and down with excitement.

"Just follow me," Rachel said. "Everything will be totally fine."

Once Alicia had checked on all the girls and seen that they were, if not tucked into bed, at least quiet and dressed in pajamas, she retreated to her room to think.

Things with Brian were not great, it was true. The day hadn't gone exactly as she'd wanted. He'd been condescending, and she'd let her temper get the best of her. Worst of all, they'd squabbled in front of the kids. That demonstrated a breakdown in leadership, and if there was one thing Alicia had learned in her teacher training program, it was that the teacher must always provide a calm, centered presence worthy of the children's trust. She hadn't felt very calm or centered when she and Brian were disagreeing. She'd felt fired up, and passionate, and really, really bothered by his attitude. He made it clear that he didn't respect her concept of the whole child, an idea grounded in her holistic approach to learning. She cared about the students—body, mind, and soul. Maybe Brian Kenner just cared about their report cards, but Alicia Deats cared about a lot more.

Then Alicia paused and looked at herself in the hotel room mirror.

"It's okay," she said to herself. "He's not really a jerk. He's just—acting like one, for some reason." Alicia had learned about "mirror work" during one of her psychology classes at Hampshire, and she found it really helpful (so long as nobody caught her doing it, as her sister had done one Christmas back home).

"You saw that he was kind back in the summer," she said to her reflection. "He took you home to make sure you were safe, and jerks don't do that. Plus, remember when he showed you his student's app, and he was so proud of the kid? There has to be a way to find that goodness in him again."

She paced back and forth and thought. Her father was a pacer, and she'd picked up the habit from him, although she really preferred to regard it as walking meditation.

She looked at the clock. It was eleven p.m. Lights out had happened an hour prior, and she was supposed to be on duty from ten until two while Brian slept. Then she'd sleep for four hours, and Brian would be on duty from two to six. Then they'd wake all the kids for breakfast and head to the Smithsonian museums.

That was the plan, anyway.

At only eleven p.m., Brian probably wasn't actually asleep yet, right? So it wouldn't matter if she went and knocked on his door and had a little chat. She wouldn't have to actually go *in* his room. She could just stand there at the door and say, "Hey, I just wanted to say, I think there was some tension between us today, and I want you to know that I'm sorry for my part in it and I wanted to re-iterate that I really respect you as a teacher and as a col-league. Tomorrow is a fresh start."

She practiced the little speech in front of the mirror, and it sounded perfectly fine and inoffensive. So she smoothed her hair and wondered briefly if she should put on makeup. She hardly ever wore makeup, preferring the natural look, but she *had* thought to bring some makeup with her that her older sister had given her at Christmas. ("It's Chanel," her sister had said. "Not that you care, but it's expensive. These are investment items. You should learn to use them." Alicia had thanked her nicely and then tossed them, un-opened, in the back of her closet in Flemington.)

"Makeup is silly," she said firmly to her reflection. "You are beautiful just the way you are." She mostly believed it, in a spiritual sense, at least.

Alicia strode confidently out the door, still wearing her T-shirt and long skirt and Birkenstocks, and went down the long hallway to Brian's room. She paused a few times along the way, cocking her head to listen for unusual sounds. But everything sounded just fine, and so she made her way to her destination. She raised her fist to knock on the door, took a deep breath, took her hand back down, turned around, and walked a few feet down the hall. Then she whipped back around and marched herself back to the door, where she knocked firmly. She heard the sounds of rustling inside and Brian's sleepy voice called, "Just a sec!" And then he opened the door, and Alicia had to restrain a gasp.

Apparently Brian had, in fact, decided to go to sleep. And apparently Brian Kenner slept in his boxers, because while he'd thrown on the robe he was still hastily tying, he hadn't quite wrapped it tight around himself. Part of it was open, and Alicia's eyes fell not just on his amazing abs but on his underwear, a pair of black boxers emblazoned with the logo for *Star Trek*.

"Whoa," Alicia murmured. "Original series."

"What'd you say?" he asked, confused. She snapped out of her reverie.

"Nothing!" she said quickly. "I just, um, I wanted to say, um—" She didn't exactly remember her speech.

"Are you okay?" he asked. "Are the kids okay?"

"Oh, yeah," she said, as if she'd forgotten the kids even existed (which she had, to be honest). "I just, um, wanted to talk to you about something."

"Come in," he said, and she followed him into his room. She noticed that all his things were very neatly laid out for the next day: boxers, undershirt, button-down shirt, slacks, shoes, socks.

"Uh—sit down?" he said uncertainly, gesturing to the desk chair. She sat down gingerly on the very edge of the chair and crossed her ankles, sitting up ramrod straight, just as she strived to do during meditation. Brian sat on the edge of one of the double beds and looked at her expectantly.

"I just—um," she said. "I just feel like maybe we didn't get along so great today, and I wanted to say that I still think you're really good at teaching and I hope we can be friends even though I know it's weird and I threw up on your dick that one time."

Okay, that wasn't exactly what she'd meant to say.

Brian looked at her for a moment and then laughed.

"Sorry," Alicia said. "That was weird."

"It was totally weird," he said, cracking up. "You woke me up to tell me that?"

"Sort of," she said.

He smiled. "Well, I mean—Alicia, it's just—let's just—let's just not even worry about the thing from the summer. That was just—it was whatever. It happened. It's over. I don't think about it ever."

"Me neither," Alicia said quickly. "Except for just now."

"Me too," Brian said.

"Cool," Alicia said.

"I was kind of an asshole to you today," Brian said, and she looked at him in surprise.

"I know how I can be," he said. "I just think you and I have different teaching philosophies, but that doesn't mean we have to disagree. I think we can figure out how to work together so our styles are complementary."

"Wow," Alicia said. "You're a lot—I don't know—easier to talk to than I thought."

"Yeah, that's what my fiancée said about me after our first date," he said, and then he seemed embarrassed.

"You have a fiancée?" Alicia asked carefully, even though she basically wanted to throw herself out a window.

"Had," he said. "Years ago."

"What happened?" Alicia asked, then clapped her hand over her mouth. "Oh my God, I'm sorry. That was like totally inappropriate of me. You don't have to tell me anything."

"I know," Brian said. "But it's okay."

"I'm just kind of a TMI person," Alicia said. "My mother says it's generational. My sister is ten years older and she says I just talk and talk and talk and it's like really unattractive."

"I wouldn't say that," Brian said, looking directly at her. "I wouldn't say that at all."

It is weird to suddenly go from wanting to die to wanting to sprout wings and do loop-de-loops in the sky, but that's how Alicia felt. Was he calling her *attractive*? Or at least not *unattractive*?

"I wish I were as social as you are," Brian said. "I see you in the teachers' lounge with all those friends. You've been here less than a year and everybody likes you. I'm just not that good at making friends. My best friends are still my fraternity brothers from MIT."

"*You* were in a fraternity?" Alicia asked dubiously.

"Yeah, but we were all nerds," he said. "I mean, it was MIT."

"We didn't have frats or sororities at Hampshire," she said.

"You don't say." He smiled at her, and she laughed a little. It came out kind of high-pitched, and she immediately turned red.

"So were you engaged at school?" Alicia asked.

"You're really direct, you know that?" he said.

"I just don't have a filter," she said. "My mother always said it was my blessing and my curse. It's how I make friends, but also sometimes I think I sound like a dork."

"Well, in answer to your question: yes. I was engaged my senior year of undergrad. She went to MIT too. Then we lived together for a year in Somerville while I was doing my masters at MIT and she was doing her masters at Harvard."

"And then?"

"And then she left me for the professor she was TAing for, and now they live together in our old apartment with a baby they adopted from Korea," Brian said matter-of-factly.

"No way!" Alicia said. "She left *you*?"

"For a women's studies professor," Brian said.

"A male women's studies professor?" Alicia said, flabbergasted. "I don't know if that's progressive or offensive. I just can't picture a guy mansplaining Audre Lorde to me."

"Oh, no, it was a woman," Brian said. "Still is, if reports

are correct. Anyway, they're happy or they probably are. I wouldn't know. I don't talk to them anymore. But yeah, that was my last girlfriend."

"You haven't had a girlfriend since then?"

"No. I've gone on dates here and there, but I was kind of burned out on dating for a few years after that."

"Jeez," Alicia said. "I can understand."

"Anyway," Brian said. "That's boring stuff. What about you? Well, you don't need a boyfriend. You're super-young."

"Twenty-three isn't super-young," she said.

"It is when you're twenty-nine," he said.

And suddenly, just like that, they were having a nice conversation. It was normal and natural and it felt really good. Alicia hoped it would go on for hours and hours.

"Tell me why you decided to be a teacher," she said, and his face lit up.

"Well," he said. "It actually started at my first Comic Con."

"This just feels like a bad idea," Gertie whispered. She and Sivan and Rachel were creeping down the hall as quietly as possible. Rachel had thrown on one of her secret outfits, purchased with babysitting money: a tiny little black tank top with spaghetti straps, a short denim skirt and a pair of platform wedges. Her hair was up in a high ponytail and the tail arched down her back like the spray from a dolphin. She wore dangly earrings and gold and silver bangle bracelets up and down one arm. For someone who was usually only allowed to wear mascara and lip gloss, she'd done an impressive job of making up her eyes in a manner that might have inspired her mother to pass out, or at least to accuse her of wanting to look like "a street corner hooker." She looked a little like a young Madonna, which is to say she appeared beautiful, confident, a little reckless, and very determined.

"Stop worrying," Rachel hissed. "Just walk like you know exactly where you're going." Man, the hallway was long.

Gertie was wearing exactly what she'd worn earlier in the day: a T-shirt and shorts. But Rachel insisted on doing Gertie's makeup, so she ended up looking like exactly what she was: a regular sixteen-year-old playing dress-up. Sivan had slicked her short hair back with some of Rachel's hair goop and put on a fresh T-shirt bearing an image of Che Guevara. Rachel and Gertie both smelled like Rachel's perfume, a knockoff brand she'd bought at Rite Aid. It was powdery and sweet. Sivan smelled like Old Spice deodorant because Sivan loved Old Spice deodorant.

Rachel was almost completely sure they were going to pull this off. Sivan was less certain, but was enjoying the rare feeling of doing something mildly dangerous. Besides, she knew her parents would almost be disappointed if she *didn't* do something a little bit rebellious on the trip. At moments, she was almost too square for their tastes. Also, they used the word "square," which was ridiculous. They were in their sixties and total ex-hippies, but still. "Square?" No thank you.

Gertie quaked with nervousness. She didn't see how she could have a good time, even if they did end up making it out of the place and back in one piece. She didn't want to drink or smoke pot or make out with a random hot boy or do anything that Rachel might want to do. She didn't much like dancing, so a club would be boring. Why were they even doing this, really? Just to say they'd done it? Just because Rachel wanted to be bad?

They reached the elevator, and Rachel pressed the down button. The elevator doors opened up almost instantaneously, and soon they were riding down to the lobby.

"See?" Rachel said simply, checking her lipstick in the elevator mirror. "Easy."

"Don't jinx it," Gertie said darkly.

"We're sixteen fucking years old," Rachel said. "They can't stop us."

"Um, they *definitely* can," Gertie said. "Need I remind you? They can put us in summer school. And put it on our permanent record."

"Okay, but besides that we're golden," Rachel said. "Stop worrying."

The elevator doors opened then, and Rachel immediately walked off through the small lobby in the direction of the entrance. Sivan and Gertie had to rush to keep up with her long-legged strides. She was walking like a runway model or something. She completely ignored the front desk staff, and they completely ignored her. There were a couple of security guards in the lobby, and they seemed similarly uninterested. The three girls glided through the entrance and out to the sidewalk like nothing was amiss, even though they were three high school students out and about at eleven thirty p.m. on a weeknight.

"See?" Rachel said brightly. "That was easy."

"I don't think we should do this," Gertie said, a little louder than she'd intended. Sivan and Rachel shushed her.

"It'll be fine," Rachel said. "We'll just figure out where we are—we can ask at the Rite Aid, it's twenty-four hours. Maybe they've got a map."

"I don't even know how to read a normal map," Gertie said.

"Didn't they teach you at camp?" Sivan asked. "They taught us at my camp. Orienteering. Basic survival."

"Your camp is different," Rachel said. "She went to, like, *Wet Hot American Summer* camp. Except not funny. It sounds kind of boring, actually. Except for the Danny Bryan part."

"Don't mention his name!" Gertie said. "It makes me feel like an idiot for not saying hi to him today."

"I still think we should go to his hotel!" Rachel said. "Let's do it. Let's go find him!"

"Go find who?" a stern voice said, and they all looked up to see a tall, muscular middle-aged man in a suit towering over them. He didn't look pleased. He wore a hotel name tag that read BOB REINA, CHIEF OF SECURITY.

"Oh, fuck," Gertie said.

"We're just going out to meet our sorority sisters at a club," Rachel said airily. "You have a good night, sir."

Bob Reina, Chief of Security, was unamused.

"Aren't you with the high school class from New Jersey?" he said, knitting his brows together and staring at each of them in turn.

Gertie felt like her heart was turning to ice. Or maybe

it was her stomach. All she felt was fear, cold and biting, inside her body.

Rachel smiled gamely.

"You know what," she said. "Maybe we won't go out after all. Maybe we'll just get some sleep before, um, our sorority meeting tomorrow at our college that we go to."

"I think you'd better follow me inside, girls," Bob Reina said with a frown. "I'm going to need to call your chaperones."

"Please don't," Gertie begged. "Please, sir. Please don't tell them."

"Just doing my job, miss," Bob Reina said. "Now let's not make this a bigger deal than it needs to be."

Sivan sighed heavily. Oh, well. At least they'd tried.

The girls followed him inside and watched miserably as he murmured a few words to a woman at the front desk. She looked up, raised her eyebrow, appeared to stifle a laugh, and then got on the phone.

"This is the worst," Gertie moaned. "My parents will kill me."

"No they won't, Gertles," Rachel said soothingly, using an old nickname from nursery school. "They'll just say something about how it's developmentally appropriate for you to do something like this at this stage. Then they'll maybe make you take the bus to school for a week instead of driving you. It's no big deal."

"You don't know," Gertie said glumly. "You don't know. I bet it'll be bad."

"Maybe they won't even tell our parents," Sivan said hopefully. "I mean, mine won't really care that much. But Rachel's will be pissed."

"Not if I tell them it really helped me reflect on the sinful nature of our nation's capital and the temptations that I face as a teenager," Rachel said. "It'll be a learning experience. They might not let me wear lip gloss for a couple months."

"I'll be super grounded," Gertie said.

"To be honest, I probably will be too," Rachel admitted. And then they waited.

Brian was in the middle of explaining his theory regarding the vital importance of cosplay at comic book conventions. Alicia was just listening, not because she didn't have a lot to say, but because she wasn't sure she was ready to say it. It was very interesting, but it was bringing up a lot of memories for her. Memories that were surprisingly still a little bit tender. She wondered if she could share them with him. She wasn't sure it was the right moment. But maybe it was.

"I think steampunk cosplay is particularly cool," Brian said. "Especially the stuff people make themselves. It's really impressive. Last year at Dragon Con down in Atlanta, there was this woman who had made a huge headdress out of antique typewriter keys, vintage ostrich feathers, and—"

The phone rang.

"Shit," Brian and Alicia said at the same time, looking at each other. Just like that, their little moment of bonding was over. It was back to teacher mode.

Brian grabbed the phone.

"This is Brian Kenner," he said anxiously. "Yes. Yes. What? Oh, Jesus."

"What is it?" Alicia whispered.

"Okay," Brian said into the phone. "We'll be right down. We're so sorry." He hung up the phone and looked at Alicia seriously.

"Sivan Finkelstein, Gertie Santanello-Smith, and Rachel Miller just got caught trying to sneak out of the hotel," he said.

"Sivan, Gertie, and *Rachel*?" she said in disbelief. "Brock Chuddford I could see. Peighton, Kaylee, and Brooklynn I could see. But those three? Really?"

"Yes, really," Brian said, irritated. "And if you'd been at your post, maybe you would've heard something."

Alicia felt stung. So that's how it was going to be? Just one little bump in the road, and boom! He was right back to throwing attitude at her?

Well, okay then.

"Let's just go downstairs," she said with a sigh. "Who caught them?"

"Chief of security."

"Oh, I hope they're not drinking," Alicia said fretfully. "Sneaking out is one thing, but—"

"Sneaking out is enough, Alicia," Brian said.

"I know that," she said. "I just hope it isn't even worse."

"We'll see," Brian said grimly. "Look, it's my fault too.

I shouldn't have kept you here talking about all this geek stuff."

"I liked it," Alicia said, but he was already halfway out the door.

They rushed downstairs to the lobby and saw the three guilty parties. Brian stalked up to them and glared at them. Alicia rubbed her forehead. She hoped she wasn't getting a migraine, but it seemed like a distinct possibility.

"Hi, Mr. Kenner," Rachel said sweetly, but her voice squeaked a little. "Hi, Ms. Deats. We were just, um . . ." She looked at Gertie and Sivan for help, but they were staring at the ground.

"We know what you were *just* doing, Rachel," Mr. Kenner snapped. "How could you violate our trust like this? This is definitely a strike one. This should be beyond a strike one. This should be strikes one, two, *and* three!"

At this, the girls looked horrified. Gertie began to cry. Sivan's eyes watered and threatened to spill over. Even Rachel choked back a sob.

"Oh, no," Mr. Kenner said, throwing up his hands. "Don't cry." He looked at Ms. Deats pleadingly. She returned his gaze and seemed to grow a little taller.

"We're very sorry about this," Ms. Deats said smoothly to the security guy, who nodded gruffly. "Thank you, Mr.—" She looked at his name tag.

"Reina," he said. "Bob Reina. Chief of security."

"Thank you, Mr. Reina," she said. "Girls, tell Mr. Reina you're sorry you tried to sneak out."

"Oh, there's no need for that," Bob Reina said, shaking his head. "It's not my rule they broke. But I'd say you folks ought to keep a closer eye on this three. I've seen this before. Kids like this—they can get up to all kinds of shenanigans."

"Absolutely," Mr. Kenner said, seeming embarrassed. "Thank you."

Ms. Deats ushered them all into the elevator, where they silently rode up. Then she marched to the girls' room and held out her hand.

"Everybody give me your keys," she said firmly, and Rachel thought she saw her shoot a little sideways glance at Mr. Kenner. He looked surprised.

Reluctantly, the girls handed over their room keys.

"You won't get these back until tomorrow night, and that's *if* I decide you've earned them back," Ms. Deats said.

The girls nodded obediently. Ms. Deats opened the door, and everyone filed into the room except Mr. Kenner, who hovered outside.

"You come in too, Mr. Kenner," Ms. Deats said.

He gingerly stepped through the door.

"Now this is a serious infraction, isn't it, Mr. Kenner?" Ms. Deats said.

"Yes it is," he said. "This is definitely a strike one at least."

"I agree," Ms. Deats said. "And to make sure this never happens again, we're going to tape your door."

"That's an excellent idea," Mr. Kenner said. Then he dropped his voice and whispered, "Do we actually have tape?" The girls totally heard him.

"I brought some in my bag," Ms. Deats said. Again, Mr. Kenner looked surprised.

"Really?" he said, and he sounded kind of impressed.

"Yes," Ms. Deats said with evident pride. "It's in my room. Patti Bump told me I should bring it just in case. She always brings tape when she chaperones."

"I never thought to do that," Mr. Kenner said. "That's a really good idea."

"I know, right?" Ms. Deats said, and grinned.

Rachel looked at Sivan and Gertie. Sivan and Gertie looked at Rachel. All three shrugged.

Awkwardly, Rachel cleared her throat. "Um, you don't have to call our parents, do you?" she asked. "Because I think mine would . . . not like it."

"I don't imagine they would like it at all, Rachel," Ms. Deats said. "If you behave yourselves and don't repeat this stunt, I don't think we need to tell your parents."

Mr. Kenner opened his mouth and then shut it without saying anything. "Whatever you say," he said.

"Now you girls get in bed," Ms. Deats said. "I'll come

back and tape your door. I don't want to hear one peep out of you for the rest of the night."

She and Mr. Kenner opened the door on the cuntriad, all clad in pajamas, looking joyful.

"Girls!" Mr. Kenner said sharply. "What are you doing out of bed?"

"We were worried," Brooklynn said. "We were scared somebody got sick. Like we did."

"Everything is fine, girls," Ms. Deats said gently. "That's very kind of you. Now go back to bed."

Brooklynn smiled over Ms. Deats's shoulder at the trio. She blew them a kiss. Then the door shut.

"That fucking bitch," Rachel said. "She loves this shit."

"They all do," Gertie said.

"How did they know we were up?" Sivan asked. "It's not like we were loud in the hallway or something."

Rachel's eyes narrowed. "They got us in trouble," she said. "I know they did it somehow."

"How?" Gertie asked. "*We* got us in trouble when that Bob Reina dude overheard us."

"Yeah, but why was the chief of security out in front of the hotel and not in some office somewhere?" Rachel said. "There were other security guards in the lobby. Why did he come out of nowhere?"

"Maybe he was walking by," Sivan said.

"Sivan," Rachel said. "You study this stuff all the time."

"What stuff?" Sivan asked.

"Rebellions," Rachel said. "Insurrections. Protests. Whatever."

"Is that what this is?" Sivan said.

"Sivan," Rachel said. "Does the Man ever just show up out of nowhere, by accident, without any information provided by a third party?"

"That's a good point," Sivan said thoughtfully. "There are informants in every movement."

"Exactly," Rachel said. "We were informed on." She walked around the room with her hands folded behind her back. Then she put her ear to the wall.

"That's Miriam and Allison's room," Gertie said to Sivan.

"Exactly," Rachel said. She raised her voice and spoke loudly, right into the wall. "AND MIRIAM AND ALLISON PLAY FIELD HOCKEY WITH PEIGHTON."

"Rachel!" Gertie was aghast. "You'll wake them up."

"Oh, they're already up," Rachel said, practically growling at the wall. "They heard everything we said and they told Peighton. I know they did." She smacked the wall.

"Maybe don't do that," Sivan said. "Somebody else could hear and complain."

"Those field hockey girls all kiss Peighton's ass," Gertie whispered. "You could be right."

"Yeah, I think she's right too," Sivan whispered. "And then Peighton called security."

Rachel stalked over to the hotel phone and pointed at a red button emblazoned with the word SECURITY.

"Look, right there. You can just call security. You can just call!" she whispered loudly. "Those bitches next door ratted us out to those cunts and then those cunts called that douchebag."

"I kind of liked Bob Reina," Sivan said. "It was kind of funny how he called out the teachers for not paying enough attention to us."

Rachel smacked her fist into her palm. Then she looked at her friends, who were a little surprised by how pissed she was.

"Let's get some sleep," she said. "They're not going to destroy our trip. But we're going to destroy theirs."

"How?" Gertie asked. "Wasn't explosive diarrhea enough?"

"I thought so," Rachel said. "But you were right, Gertie. You said they'd come back at us, and they did. So now we go on offense."

"Maybe we could just have a nice chill trip from here on out," Sivan said. "It would've been cool to sneak out, but maybe it's not meant to be."

"Which one of us is kind of psychic?" Rachel asked with a sudden smile.

"You," Gertie said.

"Allegedly," Sivan said.

"Well, I think there are great things in store for us,"

Rachel said. "I *know* there are. I just have to figure out what they are, exactly. But we're going to win this thing."

"Is it a game?" Gertie asked.

"No," Rachel said, a look of grim determination on her face. "This is war."

DAY TWO

Ms. Deats and Mr. Kenner gathered everyone in the hallway at seven a.m. and ceremoniously removed the tape from the girls' door in order to release them from what Sivan had taken to calling "our political prison." Brooklynn, Kaylee, and Peighton looked particularly delighted, and they made sure to smile brightly as the three other girls filed out into the hallway.

Breakfast at the hotel buffet was a somewhat somber affair—at least for Rachel, Gertie, and Sivan. Everyone else was thrilled because there was a waffle station with the widest array of toppings they'd ever seen. "This is like if OMG Thursdays had breakfast," Rachel heard Carter Bump say happily, helping himself to more Reese's Pieces and whipped cream.

"You know what, little bro," Brock Chuddford said thoughtfully. "That's kind of true. Why don't they have breakfast?" He looked at his lacrosse buddies as if they would have the answer. They all shrugged.

"They should," Carter Bump said. "They'd make a lot of money."

"Yeah," Brock said, nodding. Then he went to his table and Carter Bump went to his.

Over in the world of girls, things were not proceeding so harmoniously. Gertie, Sivan, and Rachel sat glumly at a table off to the side, picking at their breakfasts. Brooklynn, Kaylee, and Peighton made a big show of sitting right next to them at a neighboring table.

"You know who should sit with us?" Brooklynn asked brightly. "Miriam and Allison! Peighton, make them come here."

Peighton called their names, and the two girls scurried over, looking surprised and very happy to be included with their beloved team captain and her two BFFs. They sat down and cast a couple of nervous glances at Gertie, Sivan, and Rachel, receiving blistering glares in return.

"Nice work last night, girls," Brooklynn said to Miriam and Allison. "I mean with staying in your rooms and be-having according to school protocol and not like stupid sluts. That's what I mean. There are too many dumb whores in our grade as it is, and it's good to know you're two of the good ones."

"Just wait," Rachel said with a pretty smile.

"Wait for what, Rachel?" Brooklynn asked pleasantly. "For you to get pregnant in college and drop out?"

Rachel flipped her hair, which was a thing she only did

when she was very, very angry. Gertie and Sivan knew this, because they knew everything about Rachel, but anybody else would've thought she was just preening.

"Oh, Brooklynn," Rachel said. "Don't you know a slut is just a girl who's having more fun than you?"

"Oh, is 'fun' what you call it?" Brooklynn snickered.

"It's what Brock called it," Rachel said.

"Brooklynn!" Peighton said in a warning tone, before Brooklynn could react. "She's just trying to upset you. Don't let it bother you."

"I hope you die," Brooklynn said through gritted teeth. "I seriously hope you fucking die in like a really gross way."

"Good morning, girls," Ms. Deats said, walking up before any of them could spot her coming. She had that teacher thing where she was able to just appear sometimes when you least expected her. Mr. Kenner soon joined her.

"How's it going this morning?" Ms. Deats asked. "Peighton, Kaylee, Brooklynn? You feeling better?"

"Much better," Kaylee said brightly. "I haven't pooped in hours. I feel like totally normal."

"That's—that's great, Kaylee," Ms. Deats said. "Good to hear."

"And you girls?" Mr. Kenner said in that serious dad voice he got. "Rachel, Gertie, Sivan? Did you get everything out of your system last night?"

"I sure did," Kaylee said. "I mean, it was like—"

"K," Peighton said. "Not now."

"Yeah," Sivan said, scratching the back of her head. "I don't think we'll be doing anything like that ever again. You can count on that."

"Definitely not," Gertie said.

"We feel so stupid," Rachel said. "There have to be healthier ways of acting out our energy."

"Like, say, reading your info sheet on the National Museum of the American Indian and the National Air and Space Museum?" Mr. Kenner said. He handed out the info sheets to all the girls and moved on to distribute them to the rest of the class.

"I can't wait to learn more about American Indians," Brooklynn said brightly. "And air. And space."

"Me too!" Rachel said. "I hope we can all sit together in the planetarium. It's really exciting to see what can happen in the dark." Brooklynn looked sour.

"Well, it's nice to see you girls getting along," Ms. Deats said. "Maybe you three—Peighton, Brooklynn, and Kaylee—would even consider pairing up with Rachel, Gertie, and Sivan for your end-of-year group project. We haven't announced them yet, but they'll require a group of six."

"We'll definitely take it into consideration," Rachel chirped. "I can't wait to see what the six of us can accomplish together."

Ms. Deats smiled happily and patted Rachel on the back. Then she moved to help Mr. Kenner distribute the rest of the info sheets.

"You're a real 'see you next Tuesday,' you know that?" Brooklynn said to Rachel.

Rachel smiled.

"You can just say 'cunt,' Brooklynn," she said. "It's what I say whenever I talk about you."

Across the restaurant, Ms. Deats beamed at the girls. It was so good to see them actually having a civil discussion.

Alicia and Brian finally got to sit down to eat their own breakfast.

"I think the girls are doing well," she said, tucking into her scrambled eggs and mixed greens. "Ooh, did you know this is all local and organic? I'm really impressed with the chef."

"I don't," Brian said.

"Don't what?"

"Don't think the girls are doing well," he said. "I don't think they're getting along at all. They know how to play you."

"They do not," Alicia said, slightly insulted. "I look at them as young adults, and they respect me for that."

"They like you," Brian said. "You're fun. But that's different than respecting you."

"Oh, okay," Alicia said. "And you think they respect you?"

"I know they do."

"Maybe they fear you. And maybe that's a kind of respect. But wouldn't it be nice if they liked you too?"

"They like me," Brian said defensively. "And if they don't, I don't care."

"That's not true," Alicia said with a little smile. "You definitely care."

"I do not," he said.

"Do too," she said, and grinned at him.

"Well, maybe," he said, cracking a smile. "And I guess they do respect you a little more after that tape routine this morning. That was a good bit of theater."

"I have no idea what you mean," Alicia said innocently, popping a strawberry in her mouth. "Anyway, I did it once so I won't have to do it again."

"I wouldn't count on that, either," Brian said. "Not for one second."

"You think they'll try it again?" Alicia said. "I think we scared it out of them."

"Oh, I think they *have* to try it again," Brian said. "For their own honor."

"You're so weird," Alicia said.

"True," Brian said.

"It's kind of cute," Alicia said, to her and Brian's utter surprise.

They heard someone clear her throat then, and they looked up, startled.

"Um," Sivan said, looking at them strangely. "I think, like, we need to go to the museum now. The bus driver's here."

"Of course!" Brian said, leaping to his feet. "Yes. We were just—yes, of course." He marched off, and Sivan looked at Alicia.

"You won't sneak out tonight, will you, Sivan?" Alicia said. She dropped her voice. "It would kind of make me look bad for trusting you."

"Don't worry," Sivan said. "We're done with that."

Alicia smiled with relief.

The students poured off the bus outside the National Museum of the American Indian and stared up at it in wonder.

"Whoa," Brock Chuddford said. "That's cool as hell."

The museum didn't look like any museum any of the students had seen before. It was curvilinear, and looked almost like a smooth rock formation. There were plants and trees all over the grounds, and there was even a kind of creek flowing around the building, with a waterfall and everything. The museum didn't seem like something that had been built; it looked as if it had just grown there, somehow.

"Why's it look like that?" Brock asked nobody in particular.

"Like what?" Brooklynn asked, even though everybody knew she wasn't really supposed to talk to Brock. He ignored her and looked at his lacrosse buddies. They shrugged.

"It's cool though, right?" he said to them. They grunted their agreement. Brock looked dissatisfied. His gaze came to rest on Carter Bump.

"Yo," Brock said. "Little bro. Why's it look like that? Like, instead of normal?"

Carter Bump looked surprised again. So did Rachel, who was watching nearby.

"Why you asking that kid?" one of the lacrosse players said, sounding slightly offended that his crew's grunts hadn't been enough to satisfy Brock.

"Cuz this little dude knows a lot of shit," Brock said. "He knows about books and everything else."

"How's he know so much shit?" the other player asked, sounding genuinely curious.

"I dunno, man," Brock said. "He reads a lot. You read a lot, right, man?"

"Yeah," Carter said cautiously.

"He showed me that book I was reading last night," Brock said.

"The one that made you upset?" one of his friends said. He eyed Carter suspiciously.

"It's real sad," Brock said. "I told you, you gotta read it when I'm done."

"I will," his friend said obediently, nodding his head.

"So why's it look like that?" Brock asked Carter again, pointing at the museum.

"Well, a bunch of Native American tribes had input on how it should look," Carter said. "They all have different cultural traditions and some have different languages and religious practices, so everybody had different ideas. They finally decided they should incorporate as many native plants and grasses as possible so that the site would look like how D.C. would've looked hundreds of years ago, when only Native Americans lived here. And the building has a dome that opens up to the sky, and it's got four stones that mark the four cardinal directions."

"How'd you know all that?" Brock asked, impressed.

"It was on the info sheet they gave us this morning," Carter said.

"You actually read that?" Brock said.

"Yeah," Carter said.

Brock appeared to think for a moment.

"That's pretty cool, bro," he said. Then he walked off, and his buddies followed him.

Mr. Kenner and Ms. Deats herded the students inside, where their cultural interpreter was waiting for them. She was a beautiful young woman with long black hair that hung down her back in a single braid.

"Hi," she said to the group. "I'm Karen Begay. I'll be your guide today."

"She's so thin and pretty," Brooklynn said approvingly. "It makes me want to pay attention to everything she says."

"You know what?" Kaylee said. "I feel the same way. Like sometimes I just can't listen to ugly people for too long. They bum me out."

"She's beautiful," Peighton said.

The group moved through the exhibitions slowly, learning more from Karen than they could possibly hope to remember (well, Sivan would probably remember all of it, because she had that kind of brain). They learned about the Algonquian peoples of the Chesapeake Bay, and about the Lenni-Lenape who had lived in their own part of New Jersey. Karen taught them about the Navajo culture in which she had been raised; about the diversity of native art and handicraft; about genocide of Native Americans when Europeans colonized the Americas; about ongoing prejudice and economic hardship; about forced relocation and assimilation; and about the living Native American communities in the Americas today. There was a special exhibition on cultural appropriation, which led Ms. Deats to hide behind a totem pole and guiltily remove her dreamcatcher earrings and Tibetan prayer bead bracelet.

Eventually, it was time for the Mitsitam Café, where Karen explained they would find some of the best museum café food in the entire world, from a diverse array of native cultures found in the Northern Woodlands, South America, the Northwest Coast, Mesoamerica, and the Great Plains.

"If you want goose sausage, we've got that," she said, smiling. "Goat stew? No problem. And if you want some things that don't sound so unfamiliar, you'll find burgers and things like that too. But no matter what you eat, you must promise me you'll try the fry bread. It is the best."

Gertie, Sivan, and Rachel wandered around the café as a unit, looking at each of the five stations in awe.

"This whole place is so cool," Gertie said. "Everything about it."

"I think this is the best school trip I've ever been on," Sivan said. "Except for the part when we got caught. But like the actual school stuff has been great."

"I know what you mean," Rachel said. "I've learned so much. It makes me wish I paid more attention in social studies. And everything else, actually."

Gertie had always been an adventurous eater. Her parents couldn't afford to take her around the world, but they made sure to try different types of cooking in their home. One of the things they loved to do as a family was watch travel shows and see the kinds of foods the hosts would sample on their trips. Gertie loved photography in general but food photography in particular, and she enjoyed leafing through cookbooks and coffee table books about food. She was one of those people who Instagrams nearly everything they eat (on her real Instagram account, not her secret creeper one), but Sivan and Rachel often poked loving fun at her for *how* she did it. She always had to "style" the photos just so, and arrange everything perfectly.

She had just paid for a big tray overflowing with foods from all the represented regions when she looked up and promptly dropped it on the floor, because there, once again, was Danny Bryan. With his arm slung casually around a girl.

"Gertie!" Rachel exclaimed. "What happened?" She and Sivan rushed to help clean up the mess Gertie had made, but a café worker got there first and started collecting the broken dishware and utensils.

"I am so, so sorry," Gertie said, trying to help without taking her eyes off Danny Bryan, who had dropped his arm and was chatting with some other friend.

"Don't worry about it, honey," said another café worker. "Let's get you loaded up with food again. You won't have to pay twice."

"That's okay," Gertie said faintly. "I'm, um, not hungry anymore." And she wasn't, because *there he was*. Again. He was just sitting down to eat with a bunch of kids from Lindbergh, and that teacher they'd seen the other day.

Sivan looked in the same direction Gertie was staring.

"It's him again," Sivan said to Rachel. "Danny Bryan."

"Again?" Rachel exclaimed. "Ooh, this is great! Let's go talk to him!"

"No!" Gertie said. "No. I don't want to talk to him. He just had his arm around that girl. Look—that girl, right there." She pointed to a pretty brunette who was talking to the teacher, along with a redheaded friend. The teacher nodded, and the two girls walked off together and into the women's bathroom.

"Let's follow them!" Rachel said. "We can ask if she's his girlfriend."

"No way," Gertie said. "No freaking way."

"Gertie," Rachel said. "I like for real love you. You know this. But you've got to grow a pair."

"I don't like the way she said it, but I agree with Rachel," Sivan said.

"Oh my God, *fine*," Gertie said, throwing up her hands. "Fine. Fine! But no one is allowed to ask her if she's Danny Bryan's girlfriend. That's too weird. You just—I don't know, you have to find out somehow."

"Because that makes sense," Rachel said, rolling her eyes and laughing. The three girls took off after the older girls.

As it turned out, they didn't have to work too hard to get their answer. The two girls were just fixing their hair when Gertie, Rachel, and Sivan walked in.

"Oh my God," Rachel said brightly. "This is so weird, but aren't you the group from Lindbergh that was at the Holocaust Museum yesterday?"

"Yes, that's us," said the pretty brunette.

"We're from Jersey too," Rachel said.

"No shit!" said the redhead. "That's so cool. What high school are you at?"

"We're at FHS," Rachel said.

"What a coincidence," said the brunette.

"Yeah," Rachel said, thinking fast. "The lame part is my boyfriend is sick so he couldn't come."

"Oh, that is lame," the redhead said.

There was a pause.

"So, do you guys have boyfriends on the trip?" Rachel asked. "That must be *so* fun, I mean, if you do."

The brunette and the redhead looked a little taken aback by the oddness of the question. Gertie felt her face burning up.

"Or maybe, like, somebody you just like," Rachel added, making it weirder. "Because it'd be fun to even have a crush on somebody on a trip like this. But I totally don't. And neither do they." She gestured to her companions, who nodded mutely.

"Uh, I gotta pee," Sivan said. She fled into a stall and hid before realizing she had to actually produce pee to make this excuse sound realistic.

"I have a girlfriend," said the brunette. "But we're seniors and she's a junior, so she's not here. But I have a lot of good friends here, so it's cool."

Sivan left the stall just as soon as she'd entered it.

"Wait, you have a girlfriend?" she said excitedly.

"You have a girlfriend!" Gertie said, just as excitedly.

"Yeah," the brunette said.

"At Lindbergh?" Sivan said. "And people are like cool with it?"

"Oh, yeah," the brunette said. "It's a cool school. We're trying to start a gay-straight alliance. I think it's gonna happen too." She looked at Sivan sympathetically. "Is your school weird about that stuff?"

"Nah," Rachel said quickly, jumping in. "It's *very* accepting. So, how's your trip going?"

"It's going great, actually," the redhead said. "I worried it'd be boring but the museum yesterday was great and this museum is good too. And last night, we sneaked out of the hotel with our friends Danny and Joe and Tamra and we watched the sun rise at the Lincoln Memorial. It was fucking rad."

"Wow," Rachel said, impressed. "And you didn't get caught?"

"Nah," the redhead said. "Plus our teacher is super chill. He doesn't really care what we do as long as we don't get hurt. So even if he'd caught us, I don't think we would've gotten in big trouble. Like tonight we're partying at the hotel pool, and a couple kids brought some flasks, and I know as long as we don't make noise he's not gonna, like, stand around and watch us. He's great."

"Our hotel is sick too," the brunette said. "The Henry. The pool's open till two in the morning. Last night a bunch of us got served at the bar. It was awesome."

"Wow," Rachel said wistfully. "That's so cool. They don't tape your doors or anything?"

"What?" the redhead said. "That sounds, like, medieval."

"Okay, well, thanks for the info," Gertie said, rushing to the sink to wash her hands. "C'mon Rachel, Sivan, let's wash our hands like we came in here to do. I can't wait to try that fry bread!"

"Hey, have a good trip," the brunette said as she as the redhead walked out. "Gotta represent Jersey, right?"

"Right," Sivan said, looking at her and grinning. "Jersey strong."

The door swung shut behind the girls, and Rachel looked at Sivan.

"Did you just say 'Jersey strong'?" Rachel said. "Is that a thing I just heard come out of your mouth?"

"Shut up," Sivan said, washing her hands.

"I didn't hear you pee," Rachel said.

"I didn't actually have to pee," Sivan said. "It was just getting awkward."

"And then you found out that chick was a lesbian, and it got un-awkward."

"Whatever, Rachel," Sivan said, a little testily. "You don't know what it's like to go to school and spend all day in a place where there's no one for you to go out with even if you wanted to go out with somebody."

"Whoa, okay," Rachel said. "I didn't mean to piss you off."

"You didn't piss me off," Sivan said. "You just don't get certain things sometimes."

"I get things!" Rachel protested.

"Let's focus on the important thing," Gertie interrupted them. "Danny Bryan is single!"

"Well, he could still have a girlfriend," Sivan said.

"Sivan!" Rachel said. "Don't say that! Now who's being insensitive?"

"It's fine," Gertie said hurriedly. "It's fine, it's fine. It's no problem. Anyway, that was really good news."

"Yes," Rachel said. "Now you can go talk to him!"

"Oh, God, no," Gertie said. "Oh, no, I can't."

"Why not?" Sivan asked.

"Because I don't look good," Gertie said. "I'm just wearing these dumb shorts and this T-shirt and I didn't do anything special with my hair."

"So?" Sivan said.

"Gertie, you look beautiful," Rachel said. "I can lend you some lip gloss right now if you need it."

"No," Gertie said, trying to quell the panicky feelings rising within her. "No, I just—I better not."

"You have to!" Rachel said. "You're going to talk to him, and that's it." She made for the door, and Gertie grabbed her arm.

"No, please don't make me talk to him," she said.

"Gertie, no one's gonna make you talk to him," Sivan said.

"I am!" Rachel declared. "Maybe last night got fucked up, but *this* is going to happen. We are going to achieve at least one goal on this stupid trip. I mean, besides learning."

"I don't want to," Gertie said. "Really, Rachel. I don't want to."

Rachel looked at Gertie for a moment. Then she sighed loudly and walked out of the restroom by herself.

Gertie felt very small.

"Don't worry, Gertie," Sivan said, giving her a little hug. "She's just pissed because she got us in trouble last night. It was a dumb plan, anyway."

Gertie nodded, and the two girls left to rejoin their group. Rachel was nowhere to be seen, so they sat down by themselves and chatted awkwardly, pretending they weren't both worried about their friend's nearly unprecedented mini temper tantrum. Rachel never showed anger. Well, almost never.

Then Rachel appeared with a giant plate piled high with fry bread.

"This seriously is the best thing I've ever eaten in my life," she said through a mouthful of fried dough and honey. "You need to eat this right the fuck now."

And then, just like that, everything was okay again.

For now.

The afternoon was to be spent at the National Air and Space Museum, which was right next door to the National Museum of the American Indian. There was a moment of confusion when they were short one student in the head count, but then Peighton came hurrying after them.

"I was just asking Karen a few extra questions," she said. "I'm sorry. I didn't realize everybody had gone."

"Keep up with us, Peighton," Mr. Kenner said excitedly. "This next place is going to blow your mind."

All the students looked at each other, then back at Mr. Kenner. He *never* looked this cheerful and enthusiastic about anything, except maybe when he really got going on a lecture. But even then, he didn't look like this, all lit up and thrilled like a little kid.

"Dude is stoked," Brock observed.

"Yes, Brock," Mr. Kenner said. "This dude *is* stoked." He didn't even look mad to have been referred to as "dude."

Even Ms. Deats looked surprised.

"Wow, students," she said. "I guess Mr. Kenner is a fan of the Air and Space Museum."

"This is my favorite museum in the world," he said. "I've been to the Louvre in Paris. I've been to the Metropolitan Museum of Art in New York. I've been to the Getty in Los Angeles. I've even been to the Guggenheim Bilbao in Spain. But the Air and Space Museum has been my favorite place to visit since I was a little kid." He paused and grinned. "Just like you little guys."

The students laughed a little, which was, like, fully unprecedented because Mr. Kenner never playfully teased them. He sometimes praised them when they did a good job, but that was rare. And he hardly ever cracked jokes.

They entered the south lobby, where they reached the welcome center.

"No tour guide for this visit, gang," Mr. Kenner said. "Instead, you get this guy." He pointed to himself. "There is so much math in this building, and it's glorious. That's the best way to describe it. It is glorious."

"It is pretty great," Sivan whispered to Rachel and Gertie. "But he sounds like he's high." Rachel stifled a giggle, and Gertie coughed to hide a smile.

"In this building you'll find some of the most important examples of human accomplishment," Mr. Kenner said. "You'll see the 1903 Wright Flyer, which flew at Kitty Hawk, North Carolina, on December 17, 1903. The Wright Brothers, Orville and Wilbur, spent four years working out a prototype. And that day in December, they brought into being a dream humans had cherished since they first looked up at the sky and saw birds soaring up above. You get to *see that plane*, right here, today."

"Shit," Brock said excitedly, punching Carter Bump in the arm. He nearly sent the kid flying, but it was obviously a friendly gesture, and Carter seemed to take it as such.

"And then, a mere sixty-six years later, humanity made its first trip to the Moon," Mr. Kenner said. You could tell he was really wound up now. "Three men—Buzz Aldrin, Neil Armstrong, and Michael Collins—braved death to go on an adventure that would've been impossible if not for the flight at Kitty Hawk. You'll see their living quarters, the command module, the only part of the Apollo 11 to return to earth. You get to see that, today. You get to connect to that moment."

Mr. Kenner went on and on, growing increasingly more impassioned as he described other elements of the museum. But Gertie found her attention drifting as she looked at Ms. Deats, who seemed rapt with attention. The social studies teacher's face was shining, aglow with something Gertie recognized immediately.

"Oh my God," she whispered, almost without realizing it. "He's her Danny Bryan."

Sivan looked at her quizzically.

"Really?" Sivan said.

"Yes," Gertie said with a wistful sigh. "She's totally in love with him. I know exactly how she feels. It's like you just want to hear everything he has to say because he's so cute and smart and interesting, and you wouldn't even care if he were just, like, reciting the alphabet, because you know it would be just so awesome, and you just know the two of you were totally meant to be together."

"Fuck. That."

Sivan and Gertie turned, surprised, and looked at Rachel. She had a dark expression on her face.

"Gertie," Rachel said. "I love you? But honestly? If you don't do something about Danny Bryan, on this trip, right here in Washington, D.C., I will seriously stop being your friend."

"Yeah right," Gertie said.

"I'm so fucking serious right now," Rachel said, and she looked it. "I have been hearing about Danny Fucking Bryan for seven fucking years. And I have supported you and encouraged you and been very, very patient, and so has Sivan. But it stops now. I will block you on Facebook, Instagram, and Twitter. I will stop taking your phone calls and texts. I will delete any email you send me. I will seriously freeze you out if you don't actually, for once in your life, get up off the sidelines and get in the fucking game!"

Gertie and Sivan stared at her as if she'd grown another head.

"You have been dicking around at life for too long," Rachel said. "I'm sorry. This is tough love."

"Maybe you're just being kind of rude," Sivan suggested.

"No, Sivan," Rachel said. "I am being real. This is real life. We are grown women. In some countries we'd be married with babies by now."

"Yeah, terrible countries," Sivan said. "Like, places where women are treated like objects to be bought and sold."

"This is no time for politics, Sivan!" Rachel said. "This is about love."

"I don't see women's issues as political, per se," Sivan said. "I'm talking about human rights. And to be honest, my statement was a little First World-centric. Sometimes I need to check my privilege."

"Enough!" Gertie said. "This is dumb. Rachel, I appreciate what you're trying to do, but you and I both know you're never going to stop being my friend, and also, I just really don't want to try to talk to Danny—"

In that moment, the three of them realized the entire class was staring at them. Mr. Kenner and Ms. Deats were watching in silent amusement, their arms crossed, tapping their feet.

"Are you quite done, girls?" Ms. Deats asked.

"This is seriously the most boring fight I've ever listened to," Brooklynn said. "Like I didn't know it was possible to be so uninteresting."

"It's because it's about that one," Kaylee said, pointing at Gertie. "That one never does anything cool."

"That's Gertie," Peighton said, not in a mean way.

"Whatever," Kaylee said. "I can never remember her name."

"Let's move, people," Mr. Kenner said. "There's a lot of museum for us to hit before we're done!"

The class moved along, and Sivan and Rachel started to follow. But Gertie stood still.

"It's okay, Gertie," Sivan said. "It's not like they know who Danny Bryan is or anything."

"That's not it," Gertie said slowly. "That's not it at all. Did you hear what she said?"

"Who, Kaylee?" Rachel said. "She's so dumb, Gertles. Don't worry about her."

"She can't even remember my name," Gertie said. "We've gone to school together since she moved here in fourth grade, and she can't even remember my name. That's how unmemorable I am."

"Gertie, you need to keep in mind that she's really, really stupid," Rachel said. "And before you say anything, Sivan, I don't mean, like, challenged or disabled. That's something else entirely, and I would never make fun of that. I mean she's just stupid. She is thoughtless and selfish and stupid."

"She's right, though," Gertie said, and she began to walk slowly in the same direction as the other students. It was almost as if she were sleepwalking. Sivan and Rachel exchanged worried looks.

"What do you mean?" Sivan asked.

"I never do anything worth remembering," Gertie said as they passed a cart selling Dippin' Dots, the "Ice Cream of the Future."

"Yes you do," Rachel said soothingly. "I didn't mean to make you feel bad, Gertie. I shouldn't have done the tough love thing."

"You didn't make me feel bad," Gertie said. "Kaylee did. But in a good way."

"That doesn't make any sense," Sivan said.

"No, it does," Gertie said. "Because I'm going to do it. We're gonna sneak out tonight and we're gonna find Danny Bryan and I'm gonna tell him how I feel about him, and I don't even care if he likes me back or not."

Sivan and Rachel were silent for a moment.

"Cool," Sivan said finally. "Cool. Let's do it."

"This is going to be so awesome!" Rachel shrieked, attracting the stares of nearby patrons. She lowered her voice. "You won't regret this, Gertie, I promise!"

"I don't even care if I regret it," Gertie said. "I'm done giving a fuck about it. I give zero fucks. Like, officially. None. No fucks."

With a resolute expression, Gertie marched forward, passing underneath a banner that read TOUCH THE SKY. The other girls had to hurry to keep up.

That night at dinner, they went to a chain bar and grill called Paddy O'Flattery's that was close to the hotel, although not as close as OMG Thursdays. In fact, the original plan had been to eat at OMG Thursdays for every dinner on the trip, but the cuntriad's sickness had made that seem "imprudent," as Mr. Kenner put it.

Still high from the thrill of the Air and Space Museum, Mr. Kenner said he'd like to sit with a group of students at dinner instead of off with Ms. Deats at a teacher table for two. To everyone's surprise, Brock Chuddford's hand shot up.

"You can sit with me and my boys, Mr. Kenner," he said. "And Bump."

"Excuse me?" Carter Bump asked, clearly confused.

"You're gonna sit with me and Mr. Kenner and these bros, little dude," Brock said.

Carter Bump and Mr. Kenner looked at each other with perhaps an equal amount of wonder and walked over to Brock's table. Brock gave his buddies a hard look.

"Make room for the other dudes!" he said. "Sorry, Mr. Kenner, no offense."

"None taken, Brock," Mr. Kenner said, settling down into a chair. Carter Bump sat next to his teacher, beside Brock.

"Yo," Brock said. "Could a person fly?"

"Like in an airplane?" Mr. Kenner said.

"No, no, I mean like if I made wings to wear, like good wings with like modern materials, could I fly?" His lacrosse buddies tittered until he gave them a stern glare. Then they quieted down immediately.

"That's an interesting question, Brock," Mr. Kenner said. "I'm not sure about wings. But when I was a kid, we all thought we'd have jetpacks in the future."

"Let's say I had a jetpack," Brock said. "How high could I fly before I needed a spacesuit?"

"Well, you'd need an oxygen tank before then," Carter said. "Because the air gets thinner as you go higher."

"This kid knows everything," Brock said admiringly. "What if I had to piss while I was high up in the atmosphere?" His buddies giggled again, and again he shot them a harsh look.

"Maybe say 'urinate' instead of 'piss,' Brock," Carter Bump murmured, seeing the look on Mr. Kenner's face.

"Good call, dude," Brock said. "Sorry, Mr. Kenner. Okay. Let's say I had to urinate. Would I just, like, go? And would it just land on people down below?" He wrinkled his nose. "'Cause that sounds nasty."

"Who wants appetizers?" Carter asked. "I love fried potato skins!"

If everyone else hadn't known such a thing were socially impossible, it might've appeared that Carter Bump and Brock Chuddford were beginning to form an actual friendship. Rachel noticed, and smiled to herself.

"Please don't let Ms. Deats sit with us," Sivan whispered to Gertie and Rachel. She immediately felt guilty about it. She loved Ms. Deats, and sometimes even thought of her more as her mom's friend than as her teacher, but there was no way they could have Ms. Deats at the table if they were going to plan their great escape.

"Just don't make eye contact," Rachel said. "Let's act like we're having a really serious conversation." She put a stern expression on her face, which just made Sivan snort and Gertie crack up.

"Not helping!" Rachel said. "Not helping at all."

"Oh, look," Gertie said, sounding relieved. "She's sitting with Miriam and Allison and Olivia, over there."

"God, what a boring table," Rachel said. "We're way cooler."

"At least she's not with the cuntriad," Gertie said darkly. Peighton, Brooklynn, and Kaylee were sequestered in a booth across the restaurant, talking loudly and laughing and generally making a big show of not caring about anybody else in the group. Which of course just proved that they cared very much what everybody else in the group thought.

After their harried-looking waitress took their order and rushed on to the next table, Rachel flipped over one of the paper place mats and took out a pen. She drew a map of the hotel, the parking lot, the Rite Aid, and OMG Thursdays.

"This time we're not going out the front door," Rachel said. "We're going out the rear entrance to the first floor." She circled it on her crude map. "It's accessible from the back parking lot, but only if you have your room key. That's what we're using for our exit and our re-entry, so make sure you have your room keys on you."

"*If* Ms. Deats gives them back to us," Sivan said.

"She will," Rachel said confidently. "She wants to give them back to us. She wants to trust us. We just need to show her she can."

"And then immediately betray that trust," Sivan said.

"Right," Rachel said. "You've got it."

"Why didn't we just use the back entrance last night?" Gertie asked.

"Because I didn't know it existed," Rachel said. "Today, I studied the fire escape plan posted next to the elevator and I saw it."

"Well, that would've been a lot of help in preventing us from getting our first strike," Gertie said.

"True," Rachel said. "I'm sorry about that. It was an obvious lapse in judgment. So I'm making up for it now with this foolproof plan."

"What happens after we leave out the back?" Sivan asked.

"Next, we leave the area as quickly as possible," Rachel said.

"But where do we go?" Gertie asked.

Rachel smiled and withdrew a map from her back pocket. She unfolded it, and there was the city spread out before them.

"Wow," Gertie said. "Where'd you get that?"

"I took it from the front desk today," Rachel said. "They've just got them out there for anybody. Another thing I should've thought of last night. For someone who is probably kind of psychic, I really dropped the ball on a few things yesterday."

She circled a spot on the map. "Here's our hotel," she said. She drew a line to a neighborhood that she marked with a star. She underlined the neighborhood's name once, twice, three times.

"Georgetown," Gertie said. "What's there?"

"Bars," Rachel said. "And boys."

"But where's the Henry Hotel?" Gertie asked.

"I don't know," Rachel admitted. "I'd just look it up if we had our phones. But instead of that, I figure we can just ask in Georgetown. It's a mile away from here."

"So to be clear," Sivan said. "We're going to Georgetown just so you can hit on college boys in a college bar?"

"Yes," Rachel said. "I feel I've earned that."

"Okay," Gertie said. "But then we'll find out where the Henry is, and then we'll go right there, right?"

"Definitely," Rachel said.

"What about me?" Sivan asked.

"What do you mean, what about you?" Rachel said. "You'll be with us the whole time. We're a trio."

"Well, I'd like to do something for me, too," Sivan said. "Because we're going to a bar so Rachel can meet boys, and we're going to the Henry Hotel so Gertie can tell Danny Bryan she loves him at the pool party. But what about me?"

"What would you like to do?" Rachel said. "Anything. Anything in the whole city."

"We'll do whatever you want," Gertie said.

Sivan thought for a long moment. She'd always visited D.C. to see the museums and historical landmarks. She loved the city for that reason, for all its history and potential. She'd never thought of it as a place to hang out and be social and have adventures that didn't involve maybe being a congressional page or intern one day.

"I'll let you know," she said finally. "Nothing really comes to mind. But I'll think of something."

"Cool," Rachel said. "So we'll go to the bar, and then we'll go to the hotel, and somewhere along the way we'll do what Sivan wants to do, and then we'll sneak back in before anybody gets up in the morning, and we'll get in our beds and nobody will know we just had the best night of our entire lives. I mean, we can tell them once we've safely graduated, and then they'll all be super-jealous."

The waitress set down a platter of samosas, mozzarella sticks, and potstickers.

"Traditional Irish food," Sivan said.

"Keep eating those fried foods, girls," a voice said sweetly. Startled, they looked up and saw Brooklynn standing right there, flanked by Kaylee and Peighton.

"Really," she said. "Because your hips need more fat on them."

"Slut shaming, homophobia, and now body shaming," Sivan said. "Could you *be* more generic? At least get original with your bullshit. You're so predictable."

Gertie and Rachel stared at Sivan, surprised. So did Peighton, Kaylee and Brooklynn.

"Get out of here," Sivan said with a dismissive wave of her hand. "You're boring me."

"Whatever, loser," Brooklynn said, rolling her eyes. She and Kaylee and Brooklynn retreated to their own table.

"Sivan," Rachel said excitedly. "What's gotten into you?"

"That was pretty cool," Gertie said.

"I'm just sick of it," Sivan said with a shrug. "I hate how small they make me feel sometimes. They're not even smart enough to come up with good insults. All that shit about me being a boy, just because I don't dress like them.

Anything different than them terrifies them, so they make fun of it. I'm sick of it."

"They're disgusting," Rachel said. "But we're awesome. And we're going to have the most amazing time tonight. I guarantee it."

Back in the hotel lobby, as all the students filed in from the bus, Alicia Deats felt a hand tap her on the back. It was Sivan Finkelstein.

"What's up, Sivan?" Alicia asked. She had a lot of fondness for this kid. If any of her students were going to really do amazing things in the world, well, Sivan was the one. Babs was raising a great young woman.

"Um," Sivan said. "Well, we were wondering if it would be okay if we got our room keys back."

"Absolutely not," came Brian Kenner's voice. He strode up behind Alicia, folded his arms, and shook his head no.

Alicia felt a flash of irritation. It was *maybe* enhanced by the fact that Brian hadn't chosen to sit with her at dinner. *Maybe.*

"Now, hold on, Mr. Kenner," she said. "Sivan was speaking to me."

"She was speaking to us," Brian said. "She may have approached you, but she was speaking to both of us, through you."

"Sivan," Alicia said. "Were you speaking to me or to both of us?"

"Uh," Sivan said, looking confused. "Um, I mean, well, you're the one with our room keys, so I asked you."

"See," Alicia said. "She was speaking to me."

"Well, I am sure you agree that these girls shouldn't get their room keys back," Brian said.

"Actually, I think there's a compromise to be had here, Mr. Kenner," Alicia said. "The girls behaved exceptionally well today and I think they've learned their lesson. So my inclination is to say that yes, Sivan, you may have the keys back."

"What's the compromise?" Brian asked, frustrated. "That's no compromise."

"The compromise is that their door still gets taped," Alicia said. "One big X marks the spot."

Rachel and Gertie had been inching ever closer to Sivan, their emissary, and when they overheard this, they both gasped. Alicia and Brian stared at them.

"Will the taping really be necessary?" Rachel asked quickly.

"We're not going to sneak out," Gertie said.

"And what if there's an emergency, like a fire or something?" Rachel said. "I mean, the tape could delay us from exiting the room, and we could burn up and, you know, die."

"I doubt very much that masking tape will keep you from exiting your room in case of a fire," Brian said, amused.

"Here are your room keys," Alicia said, fishing them out of her bag and handing them to a deflated-looking Sivan. "I'll be by at lights-out to tape your door. That's at ten o'clock."

"Thanks," Rachel said, but she didn't sound thankful.

"We appreciate it, Ms. Deats," Sivan said.

"Yes," said Gertie with a little sigh. "We do."

The girls took the keys and walked away.

"I think that was good teamwork on our part," Alicia said, smiling up at Brian. But as seemed to happen with him sometimes, it was suddenly all business.

"You take the first shift, until two a.m.," he said abruptly. "I'll take the next shift. Then breakfast, then the White House, then home. Finally. Good?"

"Yeah, sure," she said.

"Good," he said, and walked off.

Alicia's shoulders slumped. It was the second and last night of the trip, and every time she felt she'd made progress with Brian, he went back to being his distant self. There was no real bonding, no real friendship. And it wasn't like he'd ever want to hang out with her outside of work after this. So, basically, the most she could hope for was a civil professional relationship that was perhaps slightly less awkward than it had been following the puke incident.

Well, all right. She'd just adjust her expectations then. Lower them.

Alicia Deats hated lowering her expectations of anyone or anything, ever. But what choice did she have?

She turned around and practically walked right into Bob Reina.

"Oh, I'm sorry, miss," he said, looking embarrassed.

"No, no, it's my fault, Mr. Reina," she said. "I wasn't looking where I was going."

"Well, neither was I, and that's no credit to a security professional," he said. "Looks like everything else is proceeding apace."

"No more complaints about my kids, I hope," Alicia said.

"Not a one," he said, smiling. "And we know how kids are—we handle plenty of school groups throughout the year. Sometimes they like to test boundaries, like those girls the other night. But they're mostly good kids at heart, I think. And you two teachers seem like you've got it together."

"I hope so," Alicia said.

"Nice they let you and your husband work the trip together," Bob said.

"Who? Oh, Brian isn't my husband," Alicia said with a little laugh.

"Your boyfriend, then," Bob said.

"Nope," Alicia said. "I don't even know if he's my friend, actually. I don't even know if he likes me at all." It was more than she'd planned to say—though that was nothing uncommon for Alicia. But there was something very comforting about Bob Reina's presence, though she couldn't put her finger on what it was, exactly. He had a kind of . . . special aura.

"Not even a friend?" Bob said. "You could've fooled me, the way he looks at you."

Alicia blushed from the top of her head to the tips of her toes. She also felt a lovely bit of hope fluttering in her rib cage.

"Oh, I wish," she said, and then blushed harder.

"You never know what can happen in Washington, D.C.," he said. "City of romance!"

Alicia laughed.

"I've never heard it called that before," she said.

"Oh, this city is full of surprises," he said. Then he smiled, gave her a little salute, and walked out the front door.

Alicia stood there for a moment in the generic hotel lobby with its unremarkable carpet and boring decorations, and something came over her. Maybe it was a burst of confidence inspired by Bob Reina's kindness. Maybe it was a second wind. Whatever it was, she suddenly knew that tonight was going to be different. Special. Better.

And how did she know that?

Because she was going to make it so.

When Gertie, Sivan, and Rachel quietly opened their door at precisely eleven p.m., exactly one hour after lights out, they found a big X of masking tape across their door. It wasn't on the door itself, as the door was set into the wall a bit. Rather, Ms. Deats had made an X across the doorframe. It was almost like a really, really basic spider web. The girls would have to walk through it to get out of the room.

"Shit," Rachel whispered. "She really did it. I thought she might forget about it."

"Why would she forget?" Gertie whispered back.

"I have this theory that she's a huge stoner," Rachel whispered back. "She probably gets high with Sivan's parents. Sivan, do you think your mom ever smokes up with Ms. Deats?"

"God, I hope not," Sivan whispered. "Look, we can do this. Check it out. She left too much room at the bottom. This is honestly kind of a shitty job on her part, not to be mean." She got down on her belly and carefully army-crawled beneath the X. She popped up triumphantly on the other side and grinned at her friends.

Gertie narrowed her eyes and furrowed her brow. Yesterday, she might've been too nervous to do it, too scared to really go for it. But tonight was a different story. Tonight she became a woman.

Gertie took off her shoes and handed them to Sivan. Then she got down on her belly and awkwardly slithered under the tape. She did it even faster than Sivan had done it. She stood up, a little red around her knees from rug burn, but triumphant.

"Wow," Rachel said admiringly. "That shoe idea was good. Here, hold my platforms." She crawled under the tape, stood up, and carefully reached through the X and pulled the door shut.

"I'm legit impressed with us," Rachel said quietly, grinning and patting her friends on the back. "Especially you, Gertie."

"She should've taped the knob and the door itself," Sivan said thoughtfully. "It was kind of a rookie move."

Sivan and Gertie were wearing their outfits from the previous evening—Sivan in her Che Guevara T-shirt; Rachel in her little spaghetti strap top. But Gertie had insisted Rachel do a full-on makeover on her, so she actually looked a whole lot older than sixteen. She was wearing Rachel's favorite secret dress, a clingy purple thing with skinny straps and a short skirt. Rachel had curled the bottom of Gertie's thick, long, straight black hair and lined her almond-shaped eyes with black liquid liner. She also did a bunch of other makeup stuff that Gertie wasn't familiar with, but it must've worked, because when Gertie looked in the mirror she almost didn't recognize herself. And that made her feel good, because she didn't want to be Old Gertie tonight. She wanted to be New Gertie, who was dangerous and reckless and who would obviously make Danny Bryan fall instantly in love with her.

Of course, even New Gertie was sensible enough to insist everyone bring a light hoodie with them just in case it got cold. Who knew how late they'd be out? And camping had taught her that temperatures could drop drastically at night and you could end up cold, so it was better to be prepared.

They walked down the hallway, the three adventurers, like champions, like commanders of their own destinies. Whether they knew it or not, they looked beautiful, and fierce, like they were ready to conquer the night. All that was missing was a wind machine and some music, and they would've made the perfect characters in some cool movie about cool teens doing cool things—until Gertie tripped over her high heels and toppled headlong onto the floor, right in front of Ms. Deats's room.

"Oh, FUCK!" Gertie said at a volume much louder than a whisper.

Rachel and Sivan froze like deer in the headlights. All three girls looked at each other, then at Ms. Deats's door.

Shit. There was no way she hadn't heard that.

They were fucked.

Alicia Deats didn't hear the giant crash right outside her door because she had her headphones in. She was Skyping on her laptop with her older sister, Danielle, a corporate lawyer in Boston. At thirty-three, blonde, and gorgeous, Danielle was married to a fellow corporate lawyer, Derek (also blond and gorgeous), whom she'd met at work. They had two adorable blond children, a loyal nanny, a full-time housekeeper/cook, and a mansion on Beacon Hill that dated to 1870. The only bad thing about their situation, Danielle was wont to say, was being Republicans in "Taxachussetts." Other than that, her life was pretty much perfect, at least to hear her tell it.

Alicia found her sister's politics detestable, her materialism deplorable, and her childrearing techniques highly problematic. Danielle and Derek thought nothing of jetting off to Paris for the weekend and leaving the children in the care of the nanny and the cook. Alicia always envisioned herself as a really nurturing, present mother who spent a lot of time with her children, teaching them organic gardening techniques and maybe doing some child-friendly weaving to encourage hand-eye coordination. Danielle was not the type of mother to mash up organic carrots into baby food or read her children a book about feelings. In fact, Danielle sometimes acted like her kids were mere accessories to her glamorous life of charity balls, international vacations, and elaborate ski trips. When Alicia saw her nieces at Christmas, she was always sure to ask them questions about their emotions, but they seemed only to want to talk about their new clothes or dolls or how good they were at ice-skating and soccer and kiddie krav maga. Alicia really hoped her own children would be more interested in abstract concepts like peace and ethics, but you never could know. Danielle's kids were like little Danielles already. They loved *things* and achievement.

Needless to say, Alicia and her sister didn't always see eye-to-eye. Alicia was not fond of confrontation, and Danielle was *very* fond of it, so their encounters often consisted of Danielle telling Alicia what she ought to do with her life, while Alicia bit her tongue and did deep breathing.

But there was one area in which Danielle had always been surprisingly helpful to Alicia, and that area was boys. It was very strange, but Danielle had kind of an empowering approach to dating. She believed that a woman should go after whatever she wanted in any area of life and that winning mattered above all else. She didn't believe in playing games unless the game would advance her own agenda. She also firmly believed that Alicia was beautiful and smart and a real catch, which was always nice to hear. Of course, she could never resist a chance to mention that one day she really, really hoped Alicia would . . .

" . . . finally get over all the hippie-dippie bullshit," Danielle said. She was wearing the headset she used at work, and her face was covered in some kind of green face mask that Alicia suspected cost an arm and a leg per jar.

"What hippie-dippie bullshit?" Alicia asked with a sigh. "Go on, I know you want to tell me."

"First of all," Danielle said. "I just really hope you start using real deodorant. You'll never get a promotion at work if you're relying on homemade crap."

"I only made my deodorant a few times, and that was in college," Alicia said.

"You're shaving again, aren't you?" Danielle asked.

"Yes, of course," Alicia said.

"Armpits and legs?"

"Yes."

"How about the bush?"

"Oh my *God*, Danielle, do we really have to talk about my pubic grooming techniques?"

"You're still doing the full bush, aren't you?" Danielle rolled her eyes. "Guys hate that. Especially guys your age. They grew up with bare pussy in porn. How many times have we had this discussion?"

"Too many times!" Alicia said. "As in, this is the third time and once was more than enough!"

"At least tell me you trim it," Danielle said. She put a cigarette to her lips and lit it. Then she inhaled.

"Danielle!" Alicia said, aghast. "When did you start smoking again? I thought you quit after law school!"

"You try to raise two children and manage a nanny and housekeeper who hate each other, plus be a perfect wife and employee and look this amazing all the time," Danielle said. "It's either have my nightly cigarette or start popping pills. And the cigarette helps me stay thin."

"Oh, Danielle," Alicia said. "A yoga practice, a whole foods diet, and plenty of water would keep you thin without giving you cancer."

"Fuck yoga," Danielle said. "It's the most boring thing I ever tried in my life. All that breathing and feeling. It's not for me. I love my spin class. All the shouting and the loud music and the feeling like you're going to puke. God, it's good."

Danielle had taken Alicia along to spin class one time. Alicia had found it absolutely terrifying. A bicycle to nowhere. She shivered at the memory.

"So anyway, this guy," Danielle said. "Personally, I think you ought to focus exclusively on men with real jobs, but that's me."

"Teaching is a real job!" Alicia said.

"I know, I know, the children are our future and all that shit," Danielle said. "I know you work hard. But teaching pays crap. If you're looking for a partner, you need one with a steady, stable income and room for growth."

"Well, whatever," Alicia said. "I'm just—I just wanted some advice on how to talk to him. I don't even know if he likes me. He acts weird around me."

"It's because he wants to fuck you," Danielle said.

"Danielle!"

"What? It's what men want. Men want to fuck women. Unless they want to fuck men. Is he gay?"

"I don't—I don't think so. I mean he had a fiancée once."

"Doesn't mean a thing. He could be queer as a three-dollar bill. I hope he doesn't cheat on you with a man."

"Danielle!"

"All right, so you want this fruit bat math teacher? I'm going to give it to you straight." Danielle took a drag on her cigarette and exhaled luxuriously. "You're going to have to fuck him."

"Danielle Deats!" Alicia was horrified. "He is not even my boyfriend yet!"

Danielle waved her cigarette dismissively. "Boyfriend, schmoyfriend. Aren't you people the ones who are always talking about free love?"

"That was hippies in the 1960s, Danielle. I am a modern woman. You know I firmly believe in monogamy so long as both partners are on board with that choice. Although I totally respect polyamory and other forms of consensual non-monogamy."

"Is that the thing where you fuck everybody else and justify it with a bunch of bullshit buzz words you learned at Burning Man?"

"That is offensive! I know plenty of poly people who—"

"Okay, whatever. I get it, your slutty hippie friends are all special flowers. But men are men are men, whether they make actual money or teacher salaries. And you're going to need to make a move on this guy. How do you think I landed Derek? I fucked his brains out."

"Not at work," Alicia said.

"Yes at work!" Danielle said. "I fucked him on his desk. Then I ignored him until he fell in love with me, at which point I made him my boyfriend. And here we are today!"

"But I'm not like you," Alicia said. "I'm not brave."

"You *are* brave," Danielle said. "You just don't know it. You've been different and gun-shy ever since that stupid geeky fucker in high school—"

"I don't want to talk about that," Alicia said hurriedly.

"Well, he fucked you over and I hate him," Danielle said. "I'd crush his fucking head if I saw him today."

"Let's focus on the present," Alicia said.

"You know, I hate to sound like a therapist, because most of 'em are cranks and thieves," Danielle said. "But I don't know if you're going to be able to move forward until you work through that old shit."

Alicia sat quietly for a moment, mulling over her sister's words.

Then there was a shriek in the background at Danielle's house, followed soon by another, higher-pitched shriek.

"Ah, fuck," Danielle said. "Both demons awaken. I have to go subdue the beasts. You take care, kiddo. You know I love you even though you're wrong about almost everything."

"I know," Alicia said. "I love you too." She shut her laptop and sat very still.

"She's right," Alicia said aloud. "And tonight's the night to do it."

It soon became evident that Ms. Deats was not going to come out and catch the girls, despite Gertie's spectacular misstep. Rachel and Sivan hauled her to her feet and took off the down the hall at lightning speed.

"Man, Gertie," Rachel said when they got to the back stairwell. "You could've ruined everything."

"Yeah, you should've taken your shoes off if you can't walk in them," Sivan said.

"Okay, so it's *my* fault I fell?" Gertie demanded. "I just tripped! It's not like I did it on purpose."

"Whoa, whoa," Sivan said. "I was just giving you some advice."

"It sounded like a criticism," Gertie said.

"It was a criticism," Rachel said. "We've got to keep our shit together so we don't get in trouble again."

The girls crept down the back stairwell quietly until they reached the first floor. Rachel gingerly opened the door to the hallway and poked her head out, looking both ways.

"Coast is clear," she whispered, and the girls emerged one by one, closing the door quietly behind them. Then they tiptoed to the end of the hallway and looked up at the EXIT sign gleaming above the back door.

"You don't think an alarm will go off, do you?" Gertie asked.

"Of course not," Rachel scoffed. Then she paused. "I mean, I don't think so."

"I hope not," Sivan said.

"Only one way to find out," Gertie said. She pushed past Sivan and Rachel and pushed the door open.

There was no alarm. Just the parking lot laid out before them like the gateway to another dimension. The street-lights glistened like stars in the firmament. Beyond, the city lights beckoned.

"Are we really gonna do this?" Rachel asked, suddenly seized by an uncharacteristic touch of anxiety.

"We sure the fuck are," Gertie said confidently. She strode out, and Sivan and Rachel followed her.

No one even noticed them leaving.

When Alicia needed to relax, she liked to put on the music of Tibetan singing bowls or a recording of sounds of the ocean intermixed with tinkling windchimes. But tonight she didn't need to relax. Tonight, Alicia Deats needed to be alert, aware, and at the top of her game. So she put on a live Fleetwood Mac album, which always got her amped. She had even brought along little speakers that attached to her laptop. She didn't blast it TOO loud, because the students were sleeping, but it was loud enough to get her blood flowing and her heart pumping.

Alicia had never quite prepared for anything like this before. She wasn't sure exactly what to do, although her sister certainly had some definite ideas about that. Speaking of which, her sister had made a big deal about her hygiene. And Alicia was a very clean, hygienic person—within reason, of course—but it was true that she hadn't taken a shower that morning. She'd been in too much of a rush to get to breakfast and to get the info sheets on the museums printed up in the hotel business center.

She *had* brought a razor . . . and her own homemade soap and shampoo and conditioner . . .

"Ah, fuck it," Alicia said, and stripped naked. She jumped in the shower and found to her surprise that it had excellent water pressure. She also found that her armpit hair was grown out maybe a bit closer to her college length than her sister would've liked. It wasn't as if Alicia had a real reason to shave her legs and armpits, so sometimes she was a bit lax. But tonight was special. Tonight she was going to shave.

She lathered up her legs while her conditioner was sitting on her hair, and she only managed to nick herself twice—pretty much a record in Alicia Deats history. As she stood up straight to rinse her legs off, she looked at her vulva, or "yoni," as they'd called it in her college Representation of Women in Art class. It was definitely in full bush mode, perhaps the fullest it had been since college. Somewhat jungle-y, even. Her first year as a teacher had been super busy and it wasn't like anyone in Flemington was actually interested in dating her, so she hadn't really given mind to what her yoni looked like. It just . . . was. And while she'd spent time in a college consciousness-raising group exploring it with a flashlight and a mirror, learning about the beautiful intricacies of the female anatomy, she hadn't even spent much time masturbating lately. She was just too tired at the end of the day, and she'd never been a masturbate-in-the-morning type of person.

It was clear to Alicia that her bush needed some pruning. Or weed whacking. She did the best she could with the razor at hand, reminding herself that feminism was about choice, and if she was making a *choice* to conform to conventional modern beauty standards, that was perfectly fine, because again, it was her body and her *choice*. She didn't shave it all off or anything. She told herself she was just trimming it back to show the property lines. *Her* property lines, of her property. Obviously.

After she was reasonably satisfied with the state of her pubic area, she rinsed out the conditioner in her hair and got out of the shower. She stood in front of the full-length bathroom mirror and scrutinized her appearance.

Overall, she was pleased with what she saw. Her boobs could've been bigger, and she could've had more of a booty, and she could be more toned, but—

"Stop it!" Alicia said to her reflection. "No body shaming allowed. I love you and you are beautiful exactly as you are." She nodded firmly and turned her attention away from superficial physical matters and on to the important question of whether she had packed any perfume. She hadn't, but her Tom's of Maine organic deodorant smelled like tea tree oil, which was pleasant enough.

Alicia hadn't brought many clothing options for a three-day, two-night trip—just the basics. Sighing, she put on a long skirt woven of hemp (it looked a little like a burlap sack but was *very* comfortable) and the tightest of the four T-shirts she'd brought, which just happened to be emblazoned with an image of the Dalai Lama. She fixed her hair as best she could, and took a moment to scrutinize the pricey makeup Danielle had bought for her the previous Christmas. She'd brought it for a reason, just in case the opportunity arose, and it seemed the opportunity was arising.

The trouble was, Alicia didn't know exactly what to do with it.

Did one put the neutral eyeshadow on and then the dramatic color over it, or vice versa? How exactly did liquid eyeliner work? And as for mascara—ugh, it made Alicia shiver just to think of it. She'd read once that there were tiny creatures, little parasites or something, at the base of the eyelashes, and they munched on mascara for fuel. She had no idea if this was actually true, but just thinking about it skeeved her out.

She settled on applying some fiery red lipstick. That would have to do. She gave herself a practice smile in the mirror, and saw that she'd already smeared the lipstick across a front tooth.

"Oh, for fuck's sake," she said, and for a moment, she sounded just like her sister.

She looked at herself in the mirror and wasn't utterly displeased. She looked nice. She looked pretty enough. Wait—did her boobs look uneven in this bra? Alicia had been self-conscious about one breast being slightly higher than the other ever since her jerky high school boyfriend— Well, there was no need to think about *that*.

Okay, vagina? Check. Hair? Check. Lipstick? Check. Boobs? Check. They stretched out the Dalai Lama's face a little, but Alicia figured His Holiness wouldn't mind.

Oh, she should definitely brush her teeth. And floss! And then brush them again, just in case. Shit, she'd have to take the lipstick off. She wiped it off quickly, and then saw that it had stained the area around her mouth. She looked like some creepy little kid who had been sucking on a cherry Popsicle for far too long. Not that any child should have a cherry Popsicle for any length of time, considering the high fructose corn syrup, but anyway. That's what she looked like.

Alicia washed her face with soap, which messed up her hair a little, necessitating some rearranging and some work with the crappy hotel room blow dryer.

And then she remembered that she didn't have any cute panties and that her bra was just boring and matched her skin tone. By the time she had brushed her teeth and carefully reapplied her lipstick, it was getting really late. And Brian was clearly asleep anyway, because this was supposed to be *her* shift.

It didn't occur to Alicia that she was doing a fairly terrible job and was shirking her duties. She was too busy wondering how to avoid getting lipstick on her teeth again. She was too busy pondering what he would say when she told him what she had to say. She was too busy feeling hot and bothered and nervous and excited.

But then, love will do that to a person.

"Georgetown," Rachel said reverently. "We made it."

They were standing at the edge of the campus, which was very pretty and had at least one building that looked like Hogwarts.

"Well, we can't get into the school," Sivan said. "So where are we going, exactly?"

"We are going to a bar," Rachel said. "And there we shall meet boys." She giggled a little. Sivan and Gertie looked at each other.

"Do we even know what the bar is called?" Gertie asked.

"Oh, there are lots of bars in this neighborhood," Rachel said, and the girls began to walk down the street.

"So which one are we going to?" Gertie persisted. "Because we can't spend all night looking for a bar here if we're going to make it to the Henry Hotel to find Danny and—"

"And do my thing," Sivan cut in.

"Which is what, exactly?" Gertie asked.

"I don't know yet," Sivan said. "I'll know it when I see it."

Gertie silently hoped Sivan just wouldn't end up finding her "thing." She loved Sivan and wanted her to be happy, but tonight was *supposed* to be about finding Danny Bryan. They were getting sidetracked as it was by Rachel's determination to get into some douche bar.

"Excuse me," Rachel said sweetly to a passing guy with a Georgetown cap. "We're looking for the best bar in this neighborhood. Can you suggest one?"

"Sure," he said with a hint of a Southern accent. "Well, it depends what you're looking for."

"Boys," Rachel said. "We are looking for boys. Hot boys, to be specific."

"Huh," he said. "Okay, well, you can go two blocks up this way and make a left and go to O'Hurley's. I don't know if the dudes are hot or whatever, but there are a lot of them. It's a frat bar."

Rachel squealed and threw her arms around the guy, who looked startled.

"Thank you sooo much," she said, and hurried off. The other girls had to rush to keep up with her.

"Do you really think they'll let us in?" Sivan asked dubiously. "We don't even have—"

"Fake IDs?" Rachel asked. "Yes, we do."

"No we don't," Gertie said.

"Yes," Rachel said. "We do." And from her purse she produced three New Jersey driver's licenses—or what *looked* like New Jersey driver's licenses.

"What the fuck?" Sivan said, her tone shocked but admiring. "You got us fake IDs! When were you gonna tell us you got us fake IDs?"

"I've been waiting the whole trip to tell you," Rachel said, looking very pleased with herself. "They're pretty great, right?"

Gertie gingerly accepted her fake ID and looked at it. It certainly looked real, and there was her face and there was a fake name, Francesca Block, and a birthdate that said she was—

"This says I'm thirty-one!" Gertie said.

"No, it doesn't," Rachel said. "I said to make it say you were twenty-one, *Francesca*."

"Who even made these?" Gertie demanded. "Where do you even get something like this?"

"The preacher's kid," Rachel said simply. Sivan and Gertie looked momentarily confused.

"You know, the one who fingered me in the graveyard," Rachel said. "The one who made me come like six—"

Gertie put a hand up.

"Rachel," she said. "We know the details. But how the hell did a preacher's kid end up getting you a fake ID?"

"Oh, it's his side business," Rachel said. "That and selling weed products. Edibles, stuff like that. As a matter of fact, I also brought—"

"Hey," Sivan said. "Mine says I'm five foot six. I'm only five feet tall."

"Whatever," Rachel said, annoyed with her friends' apparent lack of gratitude. "I worked hard to get these IDs. I had to convince my parents I wanted to go all the way to this kid's father's church over in Frenchtown. Do you know how hick Frenchtown is? It's, like, terrifying. And he still made me pay him ten dollars per ID. Granted, that's like ten percent of what he normally charges, but still. You'd think all the times I gave him handjobs in the back of camp choir practice would've counted for something."

"Apparently, they did," Sivan said dryly. "You got a two-hundred-seventy dollar discount, Rach."

"I know, but he should've just *given* them to me." Rachel pouted. They rounded a corner and saw the neon sign of O'Hurley's gleaming before them. Apparently its icon was a drunk leprechaun bent over a toilet.

"Get it?" Rachel said. "He's o'hurling." She giggled.

"How charming," Sivan said. "All right, let's get this over with."

"This is going to be fun!" Rachel said. She adjusted her boobs, flipped her hair, and walked straight up to the giant, mean-looking bouncer.

"Hi," she purred, looking right into his eyes. "Would you like to see my ID?"

He looked at her, unamused. Then he looked at Sivan and Gertie. He scowled a little and looked back at Rachel.

"Nah," he said, with a dismissive wave. "Go on in."

"You're not even going to check our IDs?" Sivan asked.

She was a little annoyed with this fellow. Underage drinking was obviously not a moral dilemma, but it was certainly a public health issue, and this man really ought to—

"She's kidding," Rachel said quickly. "We're very old. Ugh, the 90s were awesome, probably! Okay, thanks, bye!" She grabbed Sivan and Gertie and pulled them roughly behind her into the bar.

None of the girls had ever been in a bar before, and certainly not in an establishment anything like this. They were in a classic college dive bar—wood paneling with initials carved all over it; nightly pitcher specials; fraternity insignia everywhere; and, as an added touch of class, bras hanging from the ceiling. It was full of older boys—men, really—wearing Georgetown caps and fraternity T-shirts. The music was loud rock and roll of the sort Sivan was inclined to call "douche jams." Dudes were doing shots, shooting pool, laughing too loud and hitting on the pretty waitresses. There were some other girls in the place—women, really—and they were wearing tight little T-shirts and short shorts and they were flirting with the guys and, in a few corners, making out with them. As soon as the girls walked in, one shitty, loud, grating song ended, and there was a pause before the next song started up. And in that pause, which lasted about two seconds but seemed to last forever, seemingly every single soul in that place turned toward the door and stared at the little misfits who had just rolled in.

"Are they gonna kill us?" Gertie whispered to Rachel.

"Maybe," Rachel said excitedly.

"This place smells like a hate crime," Sivan said, and that's when the music started up again. Everybody went back to doing whatever they'd been doing before the girls walked in.

"What do we do now?" Gertie said.

Rachel paused for a moment and then broke into a smile.

"We do them," she said, and pointed to a table where three guys sat, apparently trying to give one another wedgies.

"No, thank you," Sivan said, but Rachel was already marching forward like a woman on a sacred mission from God.

"Hi," Rachel said brightly when she reached the table.

The guys looked up mid-wedgie and seemed pleasantly surprised.

"Hey," said one, who was a dead ringer for Brock Chuddford.

"Buy us drinks!" Rachel said.

"Rachel!" Gertie said. "That's rude. Um, guys, we're— we're sorry, she's just—"

"Hey, Tammy!" one of the guys yelled to a waitress. "Bring us a round of shots."

"You want Cuervo?" Tammy yelled back.

"Fuck no," said Not-Brock. "We want the Patron!"

"What is Patron, exactly?" Gertie asked.

Rachel looked annoyed.

"It's alcohol, Gertie," Rachel said. "God."

"It's tequila," said the third guy, who was smaller and less muscular than the other two. "You girls wanna sit down?"

Rachel slid into the booth beside Not-Brock and his friend, the one who'd called for the shots. Gertie and Sivan awkwardly sat beside Guy #3, who seemed a lot less drunk than Not-Brock and Shots Dude.

"Hi," Guy #3 said, sticking his hand out for Gertie to shake. "I'm Geoff."

"Hi," Gertie said uncertainly, and shook his proferred hand. He introduced himself to Sivan next. Rachel was immediately in deep conversation with Not-Brock, so it seemed to be left to Geoff, Shots Dude, Sivan, and Gertie to entertain themselves.

"Where you girls from?" Shots Dude asked.

"We, um, go to school here," Gertie said.

"Oh, us too," Geoff said. "What's your major?"

"Political science with a self-designed minor in Inter-cultural communications," Sivan said immediately. Gertie stared at her, and Sivan shrugged. "What? It's what I've wanted to study since I was eight."

"Sounds pretty heady," Shots Dude said.

"It is," Sivan agreed. "It's extremely . . . heady."

"I say that because I'm president of Campus Republi-cans, and even I don't know much about political science," Shots Dude said with a self-deprecating laugh.

"That doesn't surprise me," Sivan said before she could check herself. "I mean, you're a Republican."

"Oh ho ho!" Geoff said, laughing. "I see we have a Democrat at the table."

"Independent, actually," Sivan said. "I don't feel the Democratic party, as a whole, is sufficiently left-wing enough in its modern incarnation."

"Well, that's where you're wrong," said Shots Dude. "The Democratic party of today is practically the Communist party."

"I don't think you actually know what a communist is," Sivan said. "But I'd be happy to explain it to you."

And then they were off to the races, throwing jargon back and forth faster than Gertie could comprehend.

She looked at Geoff. Geoff looked at her. And they both started laughing.

"What do you study?" Geoff asked.

"Um—photography," Gertie said. "I want to be a photographer."

"I didn't even know that was a major," Geoff said. "Pretty cool. I'm pre-med."

"Wow," Gertie said. "That's really cool."

"It actually sucks," Geoff said. "I'm doing it because my parents made me. I'd rather be a social work major."

"Oh, no way," Gertie said. "My mom's a social worker. It's like super stressful. And you don't get paid enough. You'll be happier as a doctor."

"You sound exactly like my parents," Geoff said. "But honestly? I know I'd love being a social worker."

"My parents want me to be an art therapist," Gertie said grimly.

"That's so cool!" Geoff said. "I thought about that too."

"I just want to do art, though," Gertie said.

"You got any photos you can show me?" Geoff asked.

"I mean, just my Instagram," Gertie said shyly. "But you wouldn't want to see that."

"Sure I would," said Geoff, pulling out his phone, and that's when Gertie noticed three things: 1.) the shots had arrived, 2.) Geoff was very cute, and 3.) Rachel was sitting on Not-Brock's lap and giggling in his ear.

"SHOTS!" roared Not-Brock. Everybody took a glass, even though Gertie wasn't exactly sure what to do with it.

"I've never done this before," Gertie said to Geoff.

"Oh, well, you're in for a treat," he said dryly, and then laughed. "It's kind of gross. But it's worth a try. Just do what I do." So Gertie and Sivan copied him as he licked his wrist, sprinkled salt on it, and grabbed the shot.

"You lick the salt, you shoot the tequila, and then you suck on the lime real fast," he said.

"Why?" Gertie asked.

"You'll see," Geoff said.

"BOTTOMS UP!" Not-Brock yelled. And before Gertie could get too nervous, they all threw down tequila.

It felt like hot fire in Gertie's belly. It tasted fucking

gross. The lime only helped a little bit. For a moment, Gertie thought she might throw up.

"You okay?" Geoff asked with concern. "Hey, Tammy, can you bring us some water?"

"Thanks," Gertie sputtered.

Rachel, on the other hand, seemed to love it. And Sivan didn't seem affected one way or the other. She immediately went back to debating abortion law with Shots Dude.

Tammy brought the water, and Gertie downed it thankfully.

"You better?" Geoff asked. "You gonna be okay?"

"Yes," Gertie said, relieved. "Thanks."

"Let me ask you something," Geoff said. "Are you really a Georgetown student?"

Gertie was beginning to feel like it was time for some truth telling. She couldn't have said *why* she suddenly felt like sharing a few facts, but it just seemed like a good idea all of a sudden.

"No," she admitted.

"I figured," Geoff said with an understanding smile. "High school, right? Senior trip?"

"Yes," Gertie said automatically. "Yes, that's exactly it."

That's when Tammy brought another round of shots. "On the house," she said with a wink, and the three boys applauded.

"I'll pass," Gertie said.

"More for me!" said Not-Brock, and he slammed two shots. Everybody else did one—except for Gertie, of course.

"God, that's disgusting," Geoff said, wincing. "You're right to skip a second round. So is this, like, your first time in a bar or what?"

"Yeah," Gertie said. "Is it that obvious?"

"Sort of," Geoff said with a warm grin. "Hey, as long as you girls are over eighteen!"

"Why does that matter?" Gertie asked, her head swimming a little.

"Well, one, I don't think kids under eighteen are allowed in bars in D.C.," Geoff said. "And, um, your friend just went into the bathroom with my boy."

"What?" Gertie exclaimed, snapping her head back to look for Rachel. Not-Brock and Rachel were gone, but Gertie got a glimpse of Rachel's long blond ponytail from across the bar before she disappeared behind a men's room door.

"Oh, fuck no," Gertie said. "Sivan, c'mon."

"I'm sure they'll be fine," Geoff said. "He's actually in high school too. Prospective student. We figured we'd show him a good time. Just, uh, don't tell anybody I told you that."

"Okay, it's still gross," Gertie said. She pushed Sivan out of the booth and made a beeline for the bathroom. She could hear Sivan behind her, asking, "What are we doing? I was talking about voting rights legislation!"

When Gertie reached the door to the men's room, she hesitated for just a second before pushing the door in. Rachel was kneeling on the dirty tile floor, laughing and unzipping Not-Brock's jeans.

"No way, Rachel," Gertie said. "We're going."

"What the fuck are you doing in here?" Rachel demanded. "Oh my God!"

"Three on one!" said Not-Brock. "Not bad! C'mon in, ladies."

"Oh, ew," Sivan said. "Rachel, get out here."

"Oh, well, fuck," Rachel said. She got to her feet a little unsteadily. Gertie grabbed her and dragged her out the bathroom door, leaving a protesting Not-Brock behind them. They were out on the sidewalk in fifteen seconds flat.

"What exactly were you doing in there?" Gertie demanded, hustling Rachel and Sivan away from the bouncer and down the street.

"What did it look like I was doing?" Rachel said. "I was having fun!"

"Rachel, that guy was gross," Gertie said. "Sivan, wasn't he disgusting? He was a fucking date rapist."

"No he wasn't," Rachel said. "I *wanted* to blow him! And he told me he's not even in college. He goes to high school in Delaware."

"That was a dangerous situation," Gertie said. "You're too drunk to know what you're doing."

"We're not trying to be anti-sex or anything, Rachel," Sivan said mildly.

"Ugh, you two can be so fucking boring," Rachel spat.

"*What?*" Gertie said. "The whole reason we went there was because you *had* to meet boys. We didn't go there so you could go down on some stranger!"

"She's just drunk, Gertie," Sivan said. "It's good we got out of there when we did. That was a smart move on your part. Don't hold anything Rachel says against her."

The girls walked in silence for a few moments.

"Why aren't *you* drunk?" Gertie asked Sivan accusingly, aware that she was herself a bit tipsy. "You're acting normal."

"Yeah," Rachel said. "What's your secret?"

"I have a naturally high tolerance for substances," Sivan said with a shrug. "It takes something really intense to make me feel any effects."

"Speaking of really intense," Rachel said. "I have something that's gonna make you—"

"Wait, where are we going?" Sivan asked. "Stop. Let's all just stop and figure out what we're doing. Rachel, give me the map."

Rachel rolled her eyes and handed it over. Sivan cast a glance at the nearest street sign, then looked at the map. A strange gleam came into her eye.

"We're headed toward Dupont Circle," she said slowly. "It's off that way. Cool bars. Lots of stuff to do."

"Off what way?" Rachel said, confused.

"Just follow me," Sivan said. "It's just a few blocks."

Dupont Circle was not just a few blocks away. Dupont Circle was about a mile east from where they stood in Georgetown, if you took P Street NW, and Sivan knew it. Sivan also knew that Dupont Circle was a historic part of the national civil rights movement for gays and lesbians, and the site of the country's very first gay and lesbian bookstore. It was full of LGBTQ stuff. Which meant it must be full of lesbian bars.

Rachel had gotten her chance. And Gertie had already had a couple of opportunities to talk to Danny Bryan. So why shouldn't it be Sivan's turn to have fun?

"Let's go," Sivan said, and marched them off in the direction of her Sapphic destiny.

Brian Kenner's shift didn't technically begin until two a.m., and it was one a.m. when Alicia Deats finally worked up the nerve to knock on his door. She figured he could deal with it. And if he couldn't, well, they were obviously never destined to be friends or—or anything more than friends.

When he opened the door, rubbing sleep from his eyes, she barged in past him.

"What's going on?" he asked blearily. "And why do you have your laptop with you?"

"We're going to watch something together," Alicia said, sitting primly at the edge of his bed.

"Right now?" he said, confused. "Are the kids okay?"

"Probably," Alicia said, opening her laptop. "Now come here and watch this."

Slowly, he settled in beside her.

She brought up YouTube and started playing a video, *"Doctor Who Senior Thesis."*

"What the—" Brian said, then rubbed his eyes. "I mean, what the heck is—"

"Shh," Alicia said, holding a finger up. "Just watch."

He looked at the screen intently for a few seconds, then at Alicia, then at the screen, then at Alicia.

"It's a shot-for-shot remake," he said, his tone reverent.

"Shh," she said. "Keep watching."

He was right, of course. She knew he'd know what it was within a few seconds of the opening. It was a recreation of a *Doctor Who* episode—season 5, episode 10. The original episode, "Vincent and the Doctor," chronicled an adventure in which the Doctor (Matt Smith) and his companion, Amy (Karen Gillan) traveled back in time to save people from a terrible monster (the usual Doctor Who thing.) But this time, they had a very special companion in the form of Vincent van Gogh.

It was a great episode about depression, and love, and the inevitability of fate, among other things. Richard Curtis wrote it—the guy who wrote *Love Actually* and all those Hugh Grant movies. Anyway, that's not why Alicia showed this particular fan-created shot-for-shot remake of the episode to Brian Kenner. She showed it to him because—

"That's you!" Brian said incredulously. "As the Doctor!"

"Exactly," Alicia said proudly. It co-starred her then-best friend, Tallulah, as Vincent van Gogh. (Tallulah was a painter with bright red hair and soulful eyes, so it wasn't actually that much of a stretch.)

"That's my old friend Tallulah," Alicia said. "We were best friends since we were in kindergarten. This was our big joint senior thesis project. Our high school required a thesis project from each individual senior, but they let us do it together."

"And who's the dude?" Brian asked. "The guy playing Amy—who's he?"

Alicia cleared her throat.

"That," Alicia said, "Is Dirk. He was my high school boyfriend. Until he dumped me a month before graduation to be with our Dungeon Master."

Brian looked at her, his eyes wide.

"You play Dungeons and Dragons?" he asked excitedly. "Me too!"

"I *played* Dungeons and Dragons," Alicia corrected him. "Until Dirk dumped me for the Dungeon Master. The DM was Tallulah, by the way."

"Shit," he said. "That's rough. What'd you do?"

"I left," she said.

"Oh, we had a couple people leave for different reasons," he said sympathetically. "So who do you play with now?"

"I don't," Alicia said, hitting pause on the video. "We don't have to watch this whole thing."

"I want to watch it!" Brian protested. "Seriously. That's my favorite episode of the reboot."

"Mine too," Alicia said. The top of her head tingled the way it did when she had a really great yoga class.

"And you don't play anymore?" Brian asked. "That sucks. You should—" he hesitated for a moment, then plunged forward "You should play with us sometime."

Alicia's heart warmed, and she smiled brightly for a moment. But then her smile faded as quickly as it had appeared.

"Thanks," she said. "But I just would rather not even risk something like that happening again. It hurt too much. I actually, um, haven't even looked at this video in years."

"It's so good," Brian said admiringly. "I had no idea you were a Whovian."

"Was," Alicia said. "I was a big Doctor Who fan. My older sister had this boyfriend in high school who bought me the first five seasons of the reboot on DVD. But I never got past the fifth season, because . . . well . . ." She trailed off.

"What?" Brian asked, aghast. "You haven't seen any seasons since then?"

"Nope," Alicia said. "I just figure it'd remind me of that whole thing back in high school. It just seems like too much of an emotional risk."

"This was a big betrayal, huh?" Brian said, studying her face.

"Huge," Alicia said. "I lost my lifelong best friend and my boyfriend. We had all planned to go to Chapel Hill together, because we'd all gotten in even though it's really hard to get in as an out-of-state student. But after I got dumped, I called up Hampshire and asked if they'd still take me even though I'd turned them down. They said yes. So that's how I ended up at Hampshire and . . ."

"Fell in with a pack of hippies," Brian said seriously. Alicia looked at him, and he did a double-take.

"I didn't think I said that out loud," he said.

Alicia cracked up.

"You're right, though," she said. "I went full hippie. I left all my geek stuff behind me. Haven't picked any of it back up since. Until tonight."

"I'm so honored," Brian said, and he seemed genuinely touched. "Really. This means so much to me." He and Alicia locked eyes, and he smiled gently at her. Then he leaned forward.

Alicia thought she was going to faint.

"This was more than a few blocks away, Sivan," Rachel complained as they finally reached Dupont Circle. "Ugh. My feet hurt."

"But you're the high heels expert," Gertie said. "My feet feel fine."

"My knee hurts too," Rachel whined.

"Well, there's a reason for that," Gertie said, and she and Sivan giggled.

"Laugh all you want," Rachel said. "I almost got to— what base is oral? Third?"

"It's beyond bases," Gertie said. "It's not even in the stadium. It's out in the parking lot somewhere, in the back of a van."

"Well, someone's feeling sassy all of a sudden," Rachel said.

Gertie smiled. "We're getting closer to the Henry Hotel," she said. "I can feel it. All we have to do is ask somebody and take a cab there! Maybe we could even walk."

"No more walking for a while," Rachel moaned. "I need to sit down."

"We can sit down in there," Sivan said, pointing. She was illuminated from behind by a street lamp, and seemed to glow.

"There" was a bar called Sally's. It had a pretty brick exterior, and a big rainbow flag hung beside the pink neon sign. The flag fluttered gently in the evening breeze.

"In there?" Rachel asked uncertainly. "You think we'll meet more guys?"

"Nope," Sivan said happily, watching a butch woman pull the door open and enter the establishment. "Not a single one." Sivan started walking so fast the other girls had to scramble to keep up in their precarious high heels.

"Is this a lesbian bar?" Gertie asked.

"Totally," Sivan said. "Did you see that woman who just walked in? There are like a million of her inside, I bet. My people." She grinned.

That's when the same butch woman walked out and gave the girls the same hard look the bouncer had given them earlier.

"IDs," she said.

They produced their IDs quickly and waited nervously while she gave them a quick cursory glance.

"Jersey, huh?" the woman said. "Welcome to the big city, ladies. Go on in."

"This is gonna be so great," Sivan practically squealed. They walked into the bar and down a long, dark hallway to a door covered with a purple velvet curtain. Sivan paused for a moment.

"My first lesbian bar," Sivan said, almost as if she were talking to herself. "I can't believe it. I've been dreaming of this for years, and now it's finally happening."

"I've never heard her like this," Rachel whispered to Gertie. "It's kind of sweet. I just hope the lesbians don't hit on me. I hate disappointing people. I'm not homophobic. I'm just so cock oriented."

"What makes you think they'll hit on you?" Gertie whispered back. "I'm going to get all the girls." She giggled and Rachel punched her in the arm.

"*Very* sassy tonight, indeed," Rachel said. She pulled back the curtain and pushed Sivan inside. She and Gertie followed close behind, and immediately bumped into Sivan, who had stopped short.

"Oh, no," Sivan said slowly.

"What?" Rachel said, confused. "What's wrong?"

"Look around," Sivan said. "Do you see any lesbians in here?"

"I see like ten pretty girls just on that end of the bar," Rachel said. "And there's a ton more in here. So there's some guys. You can't get super mad about that. It's a free country."

"Rachel," Sivan said. "Those are not pretty girls. Those are drag queens. Look." She jerked her thumb in the direction of the ceiling, from which were suspended nine individual giant silver letter balloons that together spelled out DRAG NIGHT.

The place was packed with drag queens and with gay men bumping and grinding to the music. There was a stage on which lights flashed pink, then purple, then blue, but no one was onstage at the moment. The music thumped wildly with an infectiously catchy beat. And on a few raised platforms spread around the club, gorgeous drag queens of all shapes and sizes gyrated, bumping and grinding and vogueing. There were also some lithe young shirtless men in black booty shorts serving drinks to folks in a VIP section separated from the rest of the club by a velvet rope. The VIP section had plush chairs that looked like something out of Alice in Wonderland, and big tables for the ornate cocktails being served.

"This place is awesome!" Rachel said excitedly, clapping her hands. "This is even better than the frat bar!"

"Um, by like a million times, yeah," Gertie said, straightening her purple dress and smoothing her hair. She wanted to look very grown-up in this cool bar.

Then Rachel and Gertie looked at Sivan, whose face had fallen. She looked crushed.

"Oh my God," Rachel said. "I've never seen somebody look so depressed in the midst of such complete awesomeness."

"I was just expecting something else," Sivan said. "I just—I wanted this to be my thing. And it's great, I'm not trying to be disrespectful of a space specifically designed to celebrate homosexuality. I was just hoping the homosexuals involved would be, um, women."

"Oh, honey," said a passing waiter with a tray of empty glasses. He stopped and looked sympathetically at Sivan.

"Dyke Night is Tuesday, baby," he said.

"Thanks," Sivan said forlornly. "I'm only in town for tonight. Are there any lesbian bars around here?"

"None stupid enough to let in a high school kid, sweetie," the waiter said. He laughed when he saw the surprised look on Sivan's face.

"Don't worry," he said to the girls. "Your secret's safe with me. I grew up in Nowheresville too, and I used to sneak into the one gay club an hour away from my house. It was disgusting—I mean, Iowa, hello—but it probably saved my life."

"Oh, thank you so much," Rachel said gratefully.

"Why don't you stick around here?" the waiter asked. "We've got an empty table in VIP that we save for surprise guests. We usually reserve it for secretly gay celebrities and closeted Republican politicians, but I'm happy to comp you in. Just promise me you'll order drinks."

"We will," Gertie said, even though she didn't want to drink anything else. She just liked this guy. He was friendly and he wasn't going to get them in trouble, and that was a position she could support one hundred percent. Plus, the fact that it wasn't a real lesbian bar probably meant they'd get out of there quickly and be on their way to the Henry Hotel.

The waiter led them through the crowd to an ornate, comfy couch and settled them in.

"First round's on me, dolls," he said. "I'll be right back."

"Are we really going to drink more?" Gertie asked Sivan and Rachel.

"Yes," Sivan said grimly.

"Definitely," Rachel said. "I mean, it's free. We can always leave after the first round. But we'll leave him a big fat tip so he won't get mad at us."

"Yes, let's definitely leave after the first round," Gertie said. "We have to get to the Henry. It's super late and it's going to be a lot harder to find Danny Bryan if he's asleep."

They watched everybody dance for a few minutes, and then the waiter was back with three shot glasses, plus three limes and a little dish of salt. Three BIG shot glasses, bigger than the ones they'd seen back at the frat bar.

"I assume you babies like tequila," the waiter said, distributing the shots.

"Like is a strong word," Gertie said. "Why are these shot glasses so big?"

"Oh, these are double shots, honey," the waiter said.

"Thank you!" Rachel chirped.

"Yeah, that's cool of you, man," Sivan said.

"Um, do you know where the Henry Hotel is?" Gertie asked. "We're kind of in a hurry to—"

"Oh my God, you can't miss the drag show," the waiter said. "It's just about to start. It's amazing. A. Ma. Zing. Hurry, everybody shoot your liquor. Go! Go! Go!"

Sivan smiled a little and did a shot. Rachel cheered her on and then did a shot herself. She slammed the glass down on the table and wiped her mouth.

"Shit," she said. "All right Gertie, it's your turn."

"But I just want to know where the Henry Hotel is," Gertie said.

"I'll tell you if you take that shot," the waiter said.

"Shot! Shot! Shot! Shot! Shot!" Rachel chanted, and Sivan joined in, laughing.

Gertie took the shot.

"Oh, shit," she said as she put down her glass. "I'm gonna get real drunk, aren't I?"

"Probably," the waiter said. "But the drag show is even better when you're drunk."

As if on cue, the lights in the club dimmed.

"Oh, fuck," the waiter said happily. "She's amazing."

"Who?" Gertie asked.

"Octavia Thunderpussy," the waiter said. "She'll change your fucking life. She's even better than the queen we had last week, Regina Whore-ge."

"All right, queers," came a voice from the speaker right near Gertie's head. "Are you bitches ready for Octavia Thunderpussy?" The crowd roared its assent.

Gertie winced and moved away from the speaker.

Just then, a familiar song began. Gertie stood up very straight.

"Oh my God," she said, slurring her words. "It's 'Kids in America'!"

And it was.

That's when, from the wings of the stage, a gorgeous blonde punk rock drag queen emerged. She had a beautiful, fluffy mane of blond-and-pink long hair and wore a shredded black T-shirt and a black leather miniskirt. She had chain bracelets and sexy black boots covered in spikes. She wore what looked like a fancy bike chain around her neck.

"She's like if Dolly Parton fucked Sid Vicious!" the waiter shouted. "Yes, bitch! That is some straight Hedwig shit! Yesssss!" The girls had no idea what he was talking about, but they soon shared his enthusiasm.

Because Octavia Thunderpussy was truly amazing. She didn't just lip sync to "Kids in America," preening and posing. Oh, no. She *lived* the song, right there onstage. She was an incredible dancer, throwing in backflips and splits and all kinds of acrobatic stuff made all the more impressive by her size. She had to be at least six feet tall in those boots, and she was muscular and built, not a tiny little thing. She projected femininity and masculinity in equal measure, and she was sexy and confident and wild. Even Gertie found herself forgetting about the Henry Hotel and Danny Bryan for a moment and being swept away in Octavia's amazing energy. It was like a Broadway show and a rock concert and a million shots of tequila and a bunch of Pixy Stix full of sugar all thrown together at once. Before they knew it, the girls were on their feet with everybody else, jumping up and down and cheering.

But Octavia wasn't done after "Kids in America." She segued right into Pat Benatar's "Hit Me with Your Best Shot," which was another one of Gertie's favorite songs even though it didn't totally fit in with her usual '90s girl rocker aesthetic. Then she did Joan Jett's "I Love Rock 'n Roll," which was incredible. Octavia Thunderpussy jumped off stage while doing Roxette's "Listen to Your Heart," and walked slowly across the dance floor right to the VIP section! She serenaded (well, lip sync-enaded) the group next to them, a bunch of guys in leather who seemed thrilled by the attention.

And then, after "Listen to Your Heart," there was a pause. Octavia Thunderpussy looked at the crowd.

"Are you bitches having a good time?" she called out, breathing heavily.

"YES!" the crowd screamed.

Then she whipped around and looked right at Gertie, Sivan, and Rachel.

"But are YOU little bitches having a good time?" she demanded.

The girls shrieked and jumped up and down. They were drunk, sure, but by that point they all basically wanted to *be* Octavia Thunderpussy.

"Then get your basic little asses on stage," Octavia said, grabbing Rachel and Gertie. "I need backup dancers." Sivan cheered for her friends.

"You too, Tom Thumb," Octavia said to Sivan, who grinned and followed behind them.

"This is incredible!" Rachel screamed.

"I know, right?" Sivan yelled. "I feel like we're famous!"

"I don't know how to dance!" Gertie yelled.

"Don't worry, baby," Octavia Thunderpussy said. "Just let the music get inside you and let yourself be swept away."

She pulled them all onstage and gave them places to stand.

"Now we do a tribute to the queen herself, Miss Tina Turner," Octavia announced, and the opening strains of "Proud Mary" drove the crowd absolutely wild.

"Just follow me," Octavia told the girls. "Do exactly what I do. Got it?"

"Got it!" the three girls shouted.

What followed were the six most fun, most incredible, most exciting, and most exhilarating minutes of their lives. True to their promise, they did everything Octavia

Thunderpussy did. They moved. They shook. They kicked. They were too drunk to be embarrassed, and too happy to think about anything else that had bugged them throughout the trip—the cuntriad; their first strike; grades; Danny Bryan; anything. It was just about having fun. And there were no parents and no teachers and no judgmental classmates. There was just a giant, adoring audience that loved every single thing they did. When they finished singing about the world's most famous riverboat, Octavia brought them all up for a great big bow.

"Now get off my stage, you adorable tiny baby cunts," she said. "Javier, bring these bitches some water. They've had enough to drink for one night!"

Their waiter hurried forward and led them back to the VIP lounge, as the crowd parted and cheered for them. Then he sat them down and ran to fetch them waters. They had finally begun to catch their breath by the time he plunked down three Evian bottles in front of them.

"She *never* does that," Javier said incredulously. "Ever. Her show is all about her, and nobody else is allowed to interfere. She must've really seen something special in you girls!"

"We're pretty fuckin' special!" Sivan yelled over the noise of Octavia's closing number, Alannah Myles's "Black Velvet."

The girls were too busy guzzling water to do more than clap furiously for Octavia—no more jumping up and down for them. After the show, Javier brought Octavia a towel, and she glided through the crowd, graciously accepting the compliments from the assembled guys.

"Oh my God," Rachel said excitedly. "Octavia's coming over to us!"

The girls looked at Octavia Thunderpussy, awestruck, as she entered the VIP area and put both hands on her hips.

"Little late to be out on a school night, isn't it, babies?" she asked.

"We go to Georgetown!" Rachel said.

"And I'm a straight married man with a lovely wife and two adorable twins, Angelina and Maleficent," Octavia said, rolling her eyes.

"That's funny!" Sivan said, overcome by a fit of the giggles.

Octavia sighed and plopped down on the couch beside the girls.

"Okay," she said, and suddenly her voice changed. It became deeper, more masculine.

And it sounded kind of familiar.

"I have to say, this is pretty impressive for kids from Jersey," Octavia said. "But that doesn't mean it's okay."

"OMG," Rachel said, her eyes wide with wonder. "Are you psychic, too?"

Gertie studied Octavia's face. Beneath the layers of makeup, and the fake eyelashes, and the sparkles, and the glitter, and the glitz, and the shine, there was someone she recognized. Someone tall, and muscular, and very . . . authoritative.

"Holy fucking shit," Gertie said, her mouth dropping open. "You're Bob Reina."

Brian Kenner wrapped his arms around Alicia Deats in a warm, friendly hug. It was kind of an awkward hug, because this was Brian Kenner, after all. But it was nice. It was really nice.

They both pulled back and looked at each other a little shyly.

"So you like Dungeons and Dragons," Brian said. "Or liked, I mean."

"I still like it," Alicia admitted. "I wish I still played. Just like I wish I'd kept on watching *Doctor Who*. I feel like I gave up all my favorite things just because of some dumb boy."

"It's okay," Brian said soothingly. "We all do stuff like that. My ex—you know, the one I told you about? She used to love Thai food. And I haven't eaten Thai food since we broke up."

"But it's so good!" Alicia said.

"I know," Brian said. "It really is. I really miss it!"

Alicia had an idea. And, being Alicia, she immediately blurted it out.

"Let's order Thai food!" she said excitedly. "This is D.C. There has to be a late-night Thai place. Let's order Thai food and watch something like, um . . ."

"Like *Doctor Who*?" Brian said.

Alicia paused.

"I don't know if I'm ready for *Doctor Who*," she said.

"Well, I don't know if I'm ready for Thai food, but I'm willing to try," Brian said with a smile.

Alicia smiled back at him.

"Okay," she said. "I'll find a Thai place online if you find the sixth season of *Doctor Who*."

"Oh, I own it," Brian said. "This is easy. I was literally thinking of watching it before I fell asleep."

"No way," Alicia said.

"Way," Brian said.

They smiled at each other for longer than was absolutely necessary. And this time when Brian leaned in, Alicia knew he was going for more than just a hug.

She was right.

It was one of those kisses that felt simultaneously like the world's biggest and most electrifying fireworks explosion and the most soothing, relaxing relief. Alicia Deats felt her shoulders drop and relax for perhaps the first time since that night after Chili's. They both pulled back after a long moment and looked at each other.

"Here?" Alicia said, almost not believing it. "In the Holiday Inn?"

"We'll have to be quiet," Brian said, and they both grinned at each other.

"Like super quiet," Alicia whispered.

"Yeah," Brian said, drawing her close to him again. His hand found his way under her skirt, and Alicia was almost embarrassed at how wet she already was until she remembered that like, hello, it was completely a compliment to him, and there was no reason to be embarrassed because this was her sexual expression of—

"Oh, fuck," she moaned a little too loudly as his fingers entered her.

They looked at each other and cracked up.

"Okay, I'm going to be really quiet," she whispered. "I swear. But you're kind of making it difficult."

"I know," he said. "That's kind of the whole point."

By now he was taking her underwear off (oh God, they weren't even cute, but whatever) and her Birkenstocks and pushing her skirt up and burying his face between her legs.

"Oh my God," she said loudly again, and clapped her hand over her mouth. Without lifting his face, Brian reached out and grabbed a pillow, handing it to her. It wasn't long before she was screaming into that pillow.

It wouldn't be the last time that night. It wouldn't even be the second-to-last time. What Alicia Deats learned that night was something she'd assumed without proof in the past: Brian Kenner was really fucking good at math, but he was really fucking *great* at fucking. And to her surprise, she remembered she wasn't so bad at it herself. At one point, while her legs were practically behind her head and he was fucking her up against the headboard, she reflected that all the yoga was really starting to pay off.

"Gertie," **Rachel said.** "Who the fuck is Bob Reina?"

"The guy who caught you the other night," Bob Reina said. "I know I look a little different tonight."

"Oh, shit, you ARE Bob Reina!" Sivan said excitedly, dissolving into a fit of giggles. "No fucking way! Oh, shit! This is so cool!"

"It's not exactly cool," Bob said. "Because now we have a situation on our hands." Javier brought him a bottle of water, and he took it with a sigh.

"Oh, no," Gertie moaned, the joy of the preceding few minutes instantly evaporating. "You have to tell our teachers, don't you?"

"Oh no no no no no no no," Rachel begged Bob/Octavia, getting down on her knees and clasping her hands.

"Oh, honey, no," Bob said. "No, no, no. Have some dignity. Sit back on this couch right now."

Rachel obeyed him quickly.

"If I'd seen you on the street in my usual clothes, you bet your butts I'd have brought you right back to your teachers," Bob said, patting his elaborate wig. "But this . . . presents a complicated situation for me. If I call your teachers and tell them where I found you, everyone at work will know *how* I found you. And then they'll know what I do when I'm not at work. And I can't have that."

"Ohhhh," Sivan said. "They're like, homophobic?"

"The opposite," Bob Reina said in disgust. "They're so aggressively LGBTQIA-positive they'd all show up when I perform. And I can't have that. I don't need some annoying, boring people from work showing up and telling everybody here what a great director of security I am. My performance life is *very* separate from my work life, and I like to keep it that way." He looked around quickly and then leaned in toward the girls.

"You'd better not tell anyone here who I am," he said urgently. "Octavia Thunderpussy is mysterious, and that's why people like her. These people treat me like royalty because they have no idea what I actually do all day."

"We won't say anything," Sivan said.

"We promise," Rachel said.

"We won't breathe a word," Gertie said. "We'll just walk out of here and go about our business, and you'll just stay in here and go about your business, and nobody else will have to know."

"Well, you're almost right, kid," Bob said. "You will walk out of here and go about your business. And that means I'm going to put you in a cab and you're going straight back to the hotel."

"No!" Gertie practically shouted. "No! We have to go to the Henry Hotel! We have to see Danny Bryan!"

"Don't shout at me, missy," Bob said. "I have half a mind to just let the police scoop you up and sort things out. And if you claimed you saw the director of security at your hotel doing the most amazing drag show in the history of the art form, I would just deny, deny, deny."

"You know," Sivan said. "Some people think drag is offensive to women."

"Those people are fucking assholes," Bob said.

"Fair enough," Sivan said, impressed.

"You wouldn't call the cops on us, would you?" Rachel said, horrified.

"No," Bob relented. "I wouldn't. If only because the club would get in trouble for serving minors. I love this place. But you *are* getting in a cab, and you *are* going back to the hotel."

Gertie fought back tears. The whole night was ruined now. All her hopes of seeing Danny Bryan were dashed.

Bob walked the three drunk girls out of the club and flagged a passing cab. He put them in the backseat and gave a wad of cash to the driver.

"Take them to the Holiday Inn," he said. "And keep the change."

The cab took off, with Gertie in the backseat wedged between Rachel and Sivan.

"Whoa," Sivan said. "This night is the best."

"What are you talking about?" Gertie snapped. "This night fucking sucks."

"Gertie," Rachel said. "Count your blessings. He totally did us a huge solid. Now all we have to do is sneak back into our hotel room without getting caught. Besides, we got to do a lot of cool stuff."

"*You* got to do a lot of cool stuff," Gertie said, trying not to cry angry tears. "You got to be flirty, and Sivan got to be gay, and I didn't get to be anything!"

They were all silent for a long minute. Then Gertie leaned forward.

"Take us to the Henry Hotel," she said to the driver.

"But the drag queen said—" the driver began.

"Yes, I know," Gertie said. "And I'm saying take us to the Henry Hotel."

"That's right," Sivan said. "Take us to the Henry Hotel." She stumbled over the words and started to giggle, then shut up when she saw the determination in Gertie's face.

"Yes," Rachel said, and she slurred it a bit.

"Okay, it's your dime," the cab driver said with a sigh. He turned a corner and screeched off in another direction—for about thirty seconds.

They pulled up to a building on the same block as the gay club.

Like, seriously three doors down.

It was big and white and eight stories high and it had a big, beautiful neon sign that spelled out in pink letters THE HENRY HOTEL. Two big neon arrows pointed to it.

"Are you fucking kidding me?" Gertie exclaimed, and started giggling uncontrollably. Rachel joined her in giggling, and then Sivan went back into a giggle fit, and the driver rolled his eyes.

"You know what?" he said. "No charge. Keep the money."

"Thank yooooou!" the girls shrieked in unison, toppling out of the car and onto the sidewalk.

They lay there in a little pile laughing and squealing for a minute before helping each other to their feet.

"You ready, Gertles?" Rachel asked when they stood up tall and stared up at the building, grins plastered across their faces.

"I'm finally ready," Gertie said. "Let's fucking do this."

They strode into the Henry Hotel, confident and proud and beautiful. They looked a lot older than they were—and they also, somehow, looked very, very young.

The Henry Hotel couldn't have looked more different from the standard-issue Holiday Inn in which Flemington High School sophomores were staying. This hotel was hip and funky and cool, with lots of artsy-looking white furniture, a roaring fireplace, and a black-and-white swirly rug. Pink chandeliers hung from the ceiling. House music thumped in the lobby.

"Wow," Rachel whispered. "So cool."

Gertie marched right up to the concierge and smiled brilliantly.

"Hi," she said to the stylish young man. "We're here for a pool party."

"I'm sorry, miss," the concierge said, and he genuinely did sound sorry. "The pool closed at two a.m."

Gertie looked shocked. "It's after two a.m.?"

"It is three, miss," the concierge said gently.

"Oh, NO," Gertie moaned. "Oh this is terrible."

"Hold on," Rachel said, rushing to the counter. "Can you call a room for us? Or give us a number and we'll call the room? From, uh, your phone?"

"I'm afraid I can't unless it's an absolute emergency, miss," the concierge said. "Don't want to wake anyone up."

"It *is* an emergency!" Sivan said. "It is a huge emergency!"

The concierge looked at Gertie.

"Is it, miss?" he asked.

She sighed.

"No," she said glumly, her shoulders dropping, her eyes on the floor.

"Very well then," the concierge said. "Is there anything else I can assist you with before you're on your way?"

"We could use a cab back to the Holiday Inn," Gertie said softly. Tears pooled in her eyes and she willed them not to drop onto the pretty, fancy carpet.

"Of course, miss," the concierge said. "I'll call you one right away."

"No!" Sivan said. "There has to be some way we can get upstairs!"

"There is not, miss," the concierge said. "I can assure you our in-house security team would not permit a non-guest to enter at this hour unless a guest expressly gave permission. And now, let me call you that cab."

The girls trudged out to the sidewalk and stood under the bright green taxi light affixed to the front of the hotel. They were silent for a few minutes, Sivan patting Gertie's back and Rachel twisting her hands in frustration. When the cab arrived, they crowded into the back.

"Holiday Inn, please," Gertie said.

"No," Rachel said. "The Lincoln Memorial."

"Why?" Gertie asked.

"I know why," Sivan said. "Because Danny went, right? With the redhead and the hot lesbian and their friends."

"Exactly," Rachel said. "Sivan, sometimes we seriously do have this mind meld thing."

"No, we don't," Sivan said. "I just love you and I love Gertie and I want her to see what Danny saw too. The sunrise at the Lincoln Memorial. We can at least do that for her. Right, Gertie?"

Gertie looked very small. She sniffled.

"Okay," she said. "Let's do that, at least."

The cab driver drove off, heading south on 21st Street

NW toward the Lincoln Memorial, and the girls held hands in the backseat.

"It will be cool to see this anyway," Rachel said. "I mean, Lincoln freed the slaves."

"Only after a concerted abolitionist movement by women and people of color," Sivan interjected. "And his motivation was largely economic, not moral."

"Well, that's debatable," Rachel said.

They chattered on and Gertie half listened, bouncing along gently with the windows open to the cool night air.

He dropped them off, and it was eerily quiet but incredibly beautiful. They approached the gorgeous white marble temple with the imposing pillars, illuminated from within. Of course Sivan knew everything about it.

"Daniel Chester French designed the statue," she said in a low voice. "It's nineteen feet tall. It's supposed to be Lincoln contemplating his choices during the Civil War. Above his head, it says, 'In this temple, as in the hearts of the people for whom he saved the Union, the memory of Abraham Lincoln is enshrined forever.'"

They climbed the steps slowly and then stopped to sit on the very top step.

"This is so cool," Sivan whispered. "It's like we're sitting at his feet."

"It feels so ancient," Rachel whispered.

"Not really," Sivan said. "It was dedicated in 1922, I think."

"What do we do now?" Rachel asked.

"We wait," Gertie said. "We wait for the sun to rise. It won't be long now. Just a couple of hours." She gazed out at the vast reflecting pool and felt a kind of strange, sad peace.

They sat in silence for what seemed like forever, even though it was perhaps ten minutes at most. They all put their hoodies on, because it was the sort of cold it gets right before the dawn on any morning.

"Hey, Gertie?" Sivan finally asked, breaking the quiet.

"Yeah, Sivan?"

"What's so special about Danny Bryan, anyway?"

Gertie was quiet for a moment.

"When I look at him, I feel infinite," she said.

"Wow," Sivan said. "That's kind of beautiful."

"I don't get it," Rachel said. "Like your feelings for him are infinite?"

"Kind of," Gertie said. "It's more like the feeling I have for him, the attraction or whatever, is so strong that I feel I could power the sun or something, but forever, like it's a resource that will never run out."

"Like a renewable energy source," Sivan said. "Wind power. That kind of thing."

"Um, sure," Gertie said. "I guess. Danny Bryan is smart and handsome and funny and amazing and the idea of even being near him makes me feel like I could be happy without anything else, without us dating or having sex or getting married and having kids or anything like that. Like I could exist peacefully and joyfully just sitting near him, forever."

"So you're in love with Danny Bryan, like, for real," Rachel said.

"Yes," Gertie said. "I am completely and totally in love with Danny Bryan."

Behind them, they heard a cough. They whipped their heads around, startled.

And looked right up at Danny Bryan.

"NO fucking WAY," Rachel said.

"Holy shit," Sivan said. "Ooh boy."

Gertie said nothing. She couldn't say anything. She was in a living nightmare, and her voice froze in her throat.

He looked amazing, of course, as per usual. Perfect cheekbones. Fantastic dark hair. Dark eyes. White teeth a flash in the darkness. Good God.

"Danny *fucking* Bryan," Gertie tried to say, but she still couldn't speak.

Danny Bryan smiled down at her and practically shouted, "DO YOU GO TO CAMP WILLOPE?"

The girls looked at each other, confused.

Then Danny Bryan took out his ear buds.

"Sorry," he said in a normal voice. "I've been blasting Kendrick Lamar for like a full hour."

"Nice choice," Sivan said approvingly.

Gertie found her voice. It was very small, but she found it.

"So—you—didn't hear anything we said?" she squeaked.

"Nah," Danny Bryan said in his perfect, nonchalant Danny Bryan way. "I had the music turned way up."

Gertie looked at Sivan. Sivan looked at Rachel. Rachel looked at Gertie.

"Is this real life?" Rachel asked in wonder.

"I'm Gertie," Gertie said.

"I know," Danny said. "You're the counselor who won't ever talk to me."

Sivan and Rachel stared at each other with huge eyes. They were dying. *Dying.* And Gertie knew they were dying, but she was in such a trance that she couldn't even do anything about the fact that her BFFs were freaking out.

"I'm Danny," Danny said.

"I know," Gertie said. "You're Danny Bryan."

"Listen, I don't know if I ever did something to offend you," Danny said. "But if I did, I'm really sorry."

"Offend me?" Gertie said, shocked. "Why would you have offended me?"

"Well, you haven't said one thing to me since that day you talked to me by the salad bar your first year," Danny said. "I know it's a big camp, but that's a long time to not talk to somebody."

Gertie's world turned upside down and inside out and exploded and then came back together all in one moment.

He had thought *she* was ignoring *him.*

"It's okay, I mean, I get it," Danny said, and he sounded a little embarrassed and shy then. *Danny Bryan sounded shy and embarrassed.* "I mean when we were kids, I figured it was just because I was a couple years older and maybe you didn't want to hang out with anybody outside your level or something. But then since we've both been counselors, I always wanted to talk to you, but you'd always turn around and go the other way, or just not look at me, so, I dunno . . ."

"Oh my God," Gertie said. "I am seriously just shy. Like it's horrible. I always noticed you. I always."

It was hard to tell in the dark, but Gertie was pretty sure Danny Bryan blushed.

Danny. Bryan. Blushed.

Gertie thought she might pass out.

"Oh, shit," Rachel said worriedly. "Looks like we've got company." A crowd of about twenty figures appeared out of the darkness.

"It's cool," Danny said. "Those are my friends from school, right on schedule." As they approached and faces became clearer, Sivan saw the two girls from earlier.

"Hey!" said the pretty brunette. "We know you three! The girls from Flemington! What's up?" She laughed and hugged each of them. The redhead high-fived each of them in turn.

"What are you all doing here?" Gertie asked in wonder.

"We're here to celebrate freedom by getting fucked up and watching the sunrise," the brunette said. "Not that we aren't already fucked up. We all got kicked out of the pool for partying, actually. We had to save the night somehow, right?"

"We're wasted," the redhead said. "I mean, most of us are drunk as fuck."

"So are we!" Rachel said excitedly. "You guys brought treats, though?"

"Hell yeah we did," said the brunette.

"Awesome!" Sivan said, and she and Rachel and the other two girls ran off with some of the Lindbergh kids to get high.

Gertie and Danny Bryan stood by themselves and stared at each other. It was definitely, without a doubt, the best moment of Gertie's life on Planet Earth thus far. She didn't know if she'd ever felt so much excitement and joy all at once. She felt like she was floating. She didn't need to smoke a bowl with everybody else. No drug could possibly make her feel this awesome.

And then it got even better.

"So—hi, Gertie," Danny said, a little awkwardly. "It's nice to finally meet you."

Without thinking, Gertie stuck out her hand. And instead of shaking it, he held it.

"You promise you don't hate me?" he said, looking at her seriously.

"I don't hate you," Gertie said. "I'm just really, really shy sometimes."

"For seven years, you're shy?" Danny said.

"With you, yes," Gertie admitted. "But I always wanted to talk to you. Always."

"I get nervous around you," Danny said. "Like I'm nervous right now."

"Me too," Gertie said, and they both laughed a little.

"Well, I'm not usually shy or nervous," Danny said. "So I'm gonna hug you, okay?"

"That's probably fine," Gertie said faintly, and he wrapped her in his arms like he'd know her for years.

Which, if you thought about it, he kind of had.

They held each other for a while there, on the steps of the Lincoln Memorial, while their friends got high as hell. Gertie felt infinite.

Alicia and Brian did get around to ordering Thai food, but only after they'd fucked four times (Alicia counted the time he went down on her as the first time, the time she sucked him off as the second time, the time they did it with her legs behind her head as the third time, and the time they did it in the shower as the fourth time) and really worked up an appetite. They agreed that there was something about having sex in a hotel bed that was so much more fun than doing it in a regular bed, even though neither one of them had done it with anyone anywhere at all for quite some time. And then after pad thai, Brian suggested they watch an old rerun of *Star Trek: The Next Generation*, so they did, but then they had to fuck *again* in the middle of it.

They fell asleep naked, wrapped in each other's arms, as the black of evening gave way to the dim blue of morning.

Gertie and Danny spent the rest of the night sitting on the steps of the Lincoln Memorial, gazing out over the reflecting pool at the Washington Monument in the distance. She leaned against him and he wrapped both arms around her. It didn't feel weird and it didn't feel strange. It felt like the most normal thing in the world.

It felt like home.

"So you wanted to talk to me," Gertie said. "At camp? You really did?"

"I wanted to do more than talk to you," Danny said, and Gertie's heart leaped out of her. "You're beautiful. I always thought you were cute, but you were a little kid for so long, and then a couple summers ago you came to camp wearing this T-shirt with The Muffs on it and I love them and I was like 'Wow' and I saw how beautiful you were."

This was not happening. *This was not fucking happening.*

"Isn't it crazy that this is happening?" Danny said.

"It's bananas," Gertie said.

"Bananas is exactly what it is," Danny said.

"When do you guys go back?" Gertie asked softly. Maybe they could hang out for like days and days and days.

"This morning," Danny said. "Your hair smells good."

"Thanks," Gertie said. "I use shampoo and conditioner."

"Me too," Danny said.

"Oh, cool," Gertie said.

Sometimes you talk about stupid shit right before you kiss someone.

Danny looked at her, and Gertie looked up at him, and then—

"It's the one named Gertie!" came a voice. Gertie sat up straight, startled, and looked around.

Kaylee and Brooklynn and Peighton.

"Ooh, and her boyfriend's hot," Kaylee said.

"Thanks," Danny said, laughing, and Gertie didn't even realize that he'd basically jokingly acknowledged that they were totally and completely in love, because she was so fucking freaked out that the worst humans in the world had appeared right at the moment when she was going to experience her first kiss.

"What are *you* doing here?" Gertie hissed.

"We could ask you the same question," Brooklynn said.

"Where's Sivan?" Peighton asked.

"Is that the gay?" Kaylee asked. "I'm so bad with names."

Gertie turned and saw Rachel and Sivan hauling ass across the steps, away from the crowd of smokers.

"What are you doing?" Rachel demanded of the cun-triad. "They are obviously having a private moment. And why aren't you in bed?"

"You sound like Ms. Deats," Brooklynn said, laughing. "Relax. We're just here to have fun."

"How did you know we were here?" Sivan asked.

"Um, everybody knows you sneaked out," Peighton said. "Those walls are like super thin. So we thought it'd be a cool idea to sneak out and come here."

"It is a cool idea," Rachel said. "Which is why we had it first."

"Rachel," Brooklynn said. "Look. We're not copying you. We're copying Lindbergh High. Peighton sneaked out to use a pay phone in the lobby and called her field hockey friend who plays for Lindbergh and that girl told us about the plan to come to the Lincoln Memorial."

"A pay phone?" Danny said, confused. "They even have those anymore?"

"They do at the Holiday Inn," Peighton said, a little proudly.

"We didn't know you'd be here specifically," Brooklynn continued. "We don't like you, and you don't like us, but we were talking in our room, and Peighton was saying school is almost over for the year and we should just give up the bullshit because at best we just feel like we're better than you, which we are, and at worst, we fucking get mysterious food poisoning because we pissed you off."

Rachel hesitated for a moment.

"We know it was you," Kaylee said. "I mean it sucked but I kind of wish I'd thought of it first." She hung her head. "I never think of anything."

"It's okay, K," Brooklynn said soothingly. "It's like a pretty evil thing to think up, and we're not evil."

"I'm not sure about that," Gertie said. Having the love of your life's arms around you can make you kind of bold.

"I know we're assholes," Peighton said. "I know we don't treat you well. But you don't treat us well either. And the bottom line is, if we rat you out about tonight, you can rat us out too. So it's MAD."

"It's what?" Brooklynn asked. "I was with you till MAD."

"Mutually Assured Destruction," Sivan said quietly, looking at Peighton. "The Cold War nuclear policy of the Soviets and the—"

"—Americans," Peighton finished. "But not just them."

"You can apply it even today," Sivan said.

"Definitely," Peighton said.

She and Sivan looked at everyone else, who appeared baffled.

"Ms. Deats taught us about this just the other day," Sivan said.

"Weren't you paying attention?" Peighton asked.

"Whatever," Brooklynn said. "The point is, we're not gonna narc on you and you're not gonna narc on us."

Gertie, Sivan, and Rachel looked at one another.

"Sounds fair to me," Danny Bryan said.

"Thanks, Danny Bryan," Rachel said. "You're right."

"And who's this guy?" Brooklynn asked.

"That's Danny Bryan," Sivan said. "And those are his classmates from Lindbergh High."

"Wow, there's a lot of them!" Peighton said. "I thought it would just be the field hockey team. Let's go hang out with them." And she, Brooklynn, Kaylee, Rachel, and Sivan walked away.

Danny looked at Gertie. Gertie looked at Danny.

"I guess we should probably go hang out with everybody else," Danny said, a little reluctantly. "We can't just be a Camp Willope clique of two. I don't want to keep you from your friends."

"Of course!" Gertie said, even though she was slightly crushed. But she didn't want *him* to know that. She hopped up immediately. "Let's go."

"Oh, you actually want to?" Danny said. He sounded slightly disappointed, or maybe Gertie was just imagining that.

They walked over to the crowd, above which rose a thick cloud of marijuana smoke. Danny and Gertie coughed.

"Danny!" one of his buddies called. "C'mere, bro! You gotta check out my new pipe! It's fucking beautiful, man."

"Um, okay," Danny said. He looked at Gertie apologetically. "I'll be back in a minute."

"Sure," Gertie said, and jammed her hands in the pockets of her thin hoodie.

Rachel immediately sidled up and hissed, "OMG, Gertie, this is fucking AMAZING!!!"

"Shh!" Gertie hissed back. "We're like surrounded by Lindbergh kids. I don't want anybody to hear that I'm like this lifelong Danny Bryan fangirl."

"Oh my God," Rachel said. "Look at that." She pointed and Gertie grabbed her.

"What. The. Fuck," Gertie said, her eyes wide.

Coming down the steps, laughing like old friends, were Brock Chuddford and Carter Bump.

Shocked, Rachel ran up to them. "Brock, you didn't like kidnap Carter or something, did you?"

"Naw," Carter said before Brock could answer. "Word spread fast. We heard the mean girls were sneaking out, so we decided to come too, because it's not fair that mean girls should have all the fun. Good to see you here, Rachel." He smiled at her, and she found herself feeling a little warm inside. Must be the weed.

"We brought a few people," Brock said, jerking his thumb back.

And then, as if out of nowhere, most of the small Flemington High School sophomore class appeared. Laughing and smiling, they joined in the mix of the Lindbergh High seniors and started introducing themselves. Many of them had met on the field of battle at a lacrosse game or football game or wrestling match, but it was the first time most of them had actually said hello to one another.

"But how—" Rachel started, and Brock cut her off.

"It was Bump's idea," Brock said. "He found a bus map of D.C. and figured out we could call room to room in the hotel and tell everybody the plan. So we just took the bus here."

"Figured they can't make the entire grade go to summer school, right?" Carter said.

"The bus!" Rachel said, snapping her finger. "Dammit! We could've taken the bus. I should've thought of that." She looked at Carter Bump. "You're good, Carter," she said. "You're real good."

"Thanks," Carter said. "I'm also fucking drunk."

"Me too!" Rachel said, and they burst into giggles together.

"Nice work, bro," Brock said, and clapped Carter on the back. Then he waded into the center of the crowd, presumably to find some weed.

"So you guys are friends now," Rachel said.

"Yeah," Carter said. "But I guess weirder shit than that has gone down in this town."

"Absolutely," Rachel said. They smiled at each other for a long moment, and then Rachel did something very impulsive: she hugged him and kissed him on the cheek.

Carter hugged her back. Then at some point it stopped being a hug and started being something more. It just lasted longer than a hug would or should. He smelled really good—like really, really good. Rachel had never smelled anybody who smelled like he did. It wasn't cologne and it wasn't deodorant . . . it was just . . . him.

She looked at him and he looked at her and Rachel realized for the very first time that he had beautiful blue eyes. Without even meaning to, she moved her lips closer and closer to his—

"Hold on," Carter said, stepping back from her. "Not yet. Not here."

Rachel was shocked—both by what she'd done and by his response.

"I don't know why I just did that," Rachel said, aghast. "Or why you just did that."

"I applaud your impulse," Carter said. "But you're drunk and you don't know what you're doing."

"I do know what I'm doing," Rachel said, as she realized it was true. "I know exactly what I'm doing. And it's freaking me out."

"Look, Rachel," Carter Bump said. "I'm going to be honest with you. We both know what's going on here."

"I know," Rachel said.

"You have a crush on me," they both said at the same time.

They stared at each other.

"What?" Rachel said. "I'm not into you like that."

"Yes, you are," Carter Bump said. He wasn't being mean or snooty or cocky. He was just stating it kindly, like it was any other fact. "You have been since seventh grade science class. I dissected your frog for you. Remember?"

Rachel's brain whooshed back in time, and suddenly she was standing there, in science class, being berated by the teacher for crying because she felt so bad for the poor dead frog.

"Mr. Peck," seventh grade Carter Bump said, putting a gentle hand on seventh grade Rachel's shoulder. "It's okay that she has feelings about frogs. She's just a really compassionate person. She'll calm down."

Mr. Peck had looked at Carter. He hesitated for a moment, then his face softened. All the teachers at their middle school had a soft spot for the son of the local fallen war hero.

"You know what, Carter?" he said. "You're right. I'm sorry, Rachel. You cry all you need to. You can do the alternate assignment instead. But you have to do one of the assignments or else you get a zero."

"Th-thanks, Mr. Peck," seventh grade Rachel had said. The teacher walked away, and she looked right into Carter Bump's eyes. She smiled at him softly. He smiled back. And she felt—something. Something big. Something she didn't have a word for, exactly.

Then one of the cool soccer players hurled a dead frog that hit Carter Bump in the head, and the spell was broken.

Tenth grade Rachel was gobsmacked by the memory.

"Fucking A, Carter," she said slowly. "You're right. I must have repressed it because you're so dorky." She clapped her hand over her mouth. "I didn't mean it—I mean, I don't mean—"

"It's okay," Carter said. "I am a dork."

"But are you *my* dork?" Rachel asked, her eyes filling with drunk tears.

Carter paused and swayed back and forth for a moment. Then he caught his balance again.

"Time will tell, Rachel," Carter said. "But we have to see if we connect. I mean, I want to make out with you. I really do."

"Thank you," Rachel said.

"You're welcome," Carter said. "But I want to get to know you better first. I want to hear what you think about things."

"You do?" Rachel said incredulously. "But why?"

"Because you're you," Carter said simply, and that's when tenth grade Rachel felt the exact same thing seventh grade Rachel had felt. She smiled, and he reached out and touched her face.

And while a dead frog didn't interrupt this particular moment, something worse did: a cop.

"Hey!" yelled a police officer who popped up seemingly out of nowhere. "Hey! Hey, you kids aren't allowed to be here!"

A collective scream arose from the crowd (Brock Chuddford's scream may have been the highest-pitched of all) and they all started running. It was a stampede of stoned, drunk Jersey teenagers, and the security guard seemed more terrified than angry, but the kids were too freaked out to notice.

Carter grabbed Rachel's hand.

"RUN!" he yelled, and they did.

"But what about my friends?" Rachel yelled as their legs carried them away from the memorial.

"They'll be fine!" Carter yelled.

Gertie looked around desperately for Danny Bryan, but he was nowhere in the wild crowd. Then she turned and bumped right into him.

"Gertie!" he said. "Get out of here! I'll see you back in Jersey!"

"Okay!" she said. "Promise?"

"YES!" he shouted, squeezing her hand for a moment, and they both took off running in opposite directions.

Sivan and Peighton found themselves near each other, racing for the street. Sivan wasn't much of an athlete, and she started to lag a little.

"C'mon!" Peighton yelled, grabbing her arm and pulling her along. "We can't stay! We gotta get out of here!" Her hand slid down, and she and Sivan clasped hands. Sivan suddenly felt a new burst of energy, and she ran faster and faster, hand in hand with Peighton.

The Lincoln Memorial was clear in no time, just as the sun was rising.

Between Carter Bump's bus schedule and the surprising abundance of early morning cabs in D.C., the Flemington

High School sophomores got back safe and sound—if still drunk and high. They felt victorious. They felt like winners. They felt so amazing, in fact, that they forgot to do certain important things like brush their teeth before they caught a half hour of sleep, or take out their contact lenses, or—in the case of Gertie, Sivan, and Rachel—keep the masking tape intact.

In fact, they walked right through the tape, dizzy with love and lust and other chemicals.

"Oh, fuck," Rachel whispered. "The tape! The tape!"

"It's fine," Sivan said, the warmth and pressure of Peighton's hand still on her mind. "Ms. Deats will probably forget."

"Sivan's right," Gertie said happily. "She won't notice. Let's get some sleep."

"Okay," Rachel said, and they all flopped down onto one little double bed, clothes on, and passed out immediately.

DAY THREE

*B*EEP BEEP BEEP.

Alicia Deats woke with a start at the sound of the alarm. That's funny—her own alarm was the tinkling of windchimes. Had she accidentally set her phone alarm to some generic abrasive beep at seven a.m.?

Then she looked around.

Oh. Right.

She'd spent the night fucking the shit out of Brian Kenner.

And it had been extraordinary.

"Shit," Brian said, waking up and turning off his alarm. "Is it—oh, hi." His sleepy eyes met hers, and he smiled warmly.

"Hey, you," he said.

Alicia felt like the spirit of Etta James had entered the room specifically to croon "At Last" to both of them at that exact moment. She was over the moon. She was up in the stars, floating, so happy. She was—

"Oh, gosh!" she said, sitting bolt upright. "The kids can't see me coming out of your room! Especially not in the clothes I wore last night!"

Brian laughed.

"You're not exactly in any clothes right now," he pointed out.

"Thank you," Alicia said, hitting him with a pillow. "Very helpful."

"Oh, they're not up yet," he said, batting the pillow away. "I think you're good. If anyone sees you, we can just say we had a very important early morning meeting. In my hotel room. Alone." They both giggled and blushed.

"Okay, well, um," Alicia said, struggling to get into her clothes. She gathered her laptop and smoothed her hair. "Um. Thank you for a very nice evening. And I guess I will see you at breakfast."

"I guess you will," he said, flashing that perfect grin, and she almost melted into a puddle right there on the spot.

She peered cautiously out the door before actually moving into the hallway. No kids. Not one.

Relieved, she tiptoed into the hallway, quietly closing the door behind her. She moved stealthily down the hall, like some kind of hippie ninja, and was not too far from her door when something caught her eye.

The tape on the girls' door.

It was broken.

Alicia felt her heart drop. Oh, God. The girls had sneaked out *again*. Were they home? Were they safe?

She paused and cocked her ear. She could hear light snoring from within the room. Relieved, she let her shoulders drop.

And that's when she got angry.

She had been the one to fight for them. She had been the one to give them chances. And now they abused her trust like this—again?

No *fucking* way.

Sure, she was high off a night of great sex, but that didn't mean she couldn't snap right back into teacher mode.

Alicia Deats had hit her limit.

She banged on the door louder than she'd ever banged on a door before. She didn't just do it once or twice or even three times. She kept doing it, loud and insistent, until finally she heard someone move toward the door. She stopped only when Sivan actually physically opened the door.

Alicia narrowed her eyes and stared down into Sivan's guilty face.

"You lied to me," she said. She didn't shout it, but she said it pretty loudly. As she'd already woken the floor up with banging on the door, it was no surprise that heads began poking out of doors up and down the hall.

"N-no I didn't," Sivan said, staring at the floor.

"Yes you did," Alicia said. "I put my trust in you, and you lied to me. And now you're lying about lying. *Where* did you go last night?"

"Um . . ." Sivan said. "Uh . . ."

The other two girls rushed up behind her. At the same time, Brian hurried to see what was going on.

"Nowhere!" Rachel said quickly. "Well, I mean, we went somewhere. We were—we were—"

"We were so moved by what we saw at the American Indian Museum," Gertie said. "You know, the Trail of Tears part? Anyway, we were really upset. So we went down to the lobby to talk about our feelings."

"You went down to the lobby to talk about your feelings," Alicia repeated slowly. "And you expect me to believe that?"

"We just needed a change of scenery," Rachel said. "Brighter colors, people moving around. We knew it was wrong and we felt bad but we just—needed to cheer up. That's as far as we went. We didn't leave the hotel."

"We definitely didn't leave the hotel," Sivan said, nodding vigorously.

"I do not believe you went down to the lobby to talk about your feelings," Alicia said. "And why are you all dressed up like that? You're going to tell me you got up to talk about your feelings, then came back to bed, slept, woke up, and got fully made up and dressed up for a trip to the White House? Already? I don't believe you for one minute. Especially about the feelings part."

"I do," said Brian. Everyone looked at him, shocked.

"Feelings can be . . . complicated," Brian continued. "Sometimes it takes talking it out for a while before the feelings start to make sense."

Alicia looked at him and felt warm and sweet inside again. He looked back at her. They both smiled.

Sivan looked at Rachel. Rachel looked at Sivan. Gertie looked at Alicia and Brian.

"Oh," she said quietly, recognizing what passed between them.

"Oh, what?" Alicia asked, snapping back to attention.

"Oh . . . we were wrong," Gertie said. "We know we were wrong. And we're really sorry."

"Well, this is your second strike," Alicia said.

The girls gasped.

"She's right," Brian said. "This is your second strike. It's good that you didn't go far and we know you didn't mean any harm by it. But rules are rules. Just behave perfectly the rest of the trip and we won't have to talk about summer school." He paused. "We won't even have to tell your parents. Again, unless there's a strike three."

"There won't be," Rachel said. "We promise. Thank you so much. We'll get ready for breakfast now."

"So will I," Alicia said, and it was then that the girls

noticed she was wearing the same clothes as the previous day.

Alicia noticed them noticing.

"I, uh," Alicia said. "I stayed up reading Noam Chomsky all night." The girls nodded as if this were a perfectly normal thing to say, apropos of nothing.

Alicia rushed off to her room, leaving thoughts of the girls behind her momentarily. She needed to shower. She needed to put on fresh clothes. And she needed to reconsider trying to put on some of that makeup her sister had given her. Because of Brian. Who was so cute, and so handsome, and so sexy, and smelled so good up close.

She stripped quickly and jumped in the shower. As the hot water hit her skin, she reflected that maybe now was a decent time to reconsider that whole no-masturbating-in-the-morning thing.

After all, it was a stress reliever, right?

Everyone who'd gone out that night was hung over. Of the trio of girls, Gertie was by far in the worst shape. Gertie puked twice before they left for breakfast. She reflected that she would never, ever, ever drink tequila ever again if this was what it did to you.

The whole grade got to breakfast early, and the buffet hadn't officially opened yet. As the food workers bustled about preparing everything, Rachel, Gertie, and Sivan held their stomachs.

"I'm starving," Rachel moaned.

"How can I be so hungry when I'm so fucking nauseous?" Gertie groaned.

"I honestly don't feel that bad," Sivan said.

"Let me see if I have any Tic Tacs or whatever," Rachel said, and she opened her purse. A Ziploc baggie with three cookies fell out.

"Fuck yes!" Gertie said, grabbing the bag. She pulled out a cookie and pitched the other to Sivan, who caught it happily.

"Wait—" Rachel protested, but they were already shoving the cookies in their mouths.

"This is so good," Sivan said.

"Oh my God," Gertie said. "I loooove this. Thanks, Rachel."

"Oh, boy," Rachel said. "Oh, boy."

"Aren't you gonna eat one?" Gertie asked through a mouthful of cookie.

"Um," Rachel said. "Sure." She took a tiny bite, barely even a crumb, and pretended to chew it. Ms. Deats saw what was happening and walked over.

"Rachel," Ms. Deats said. "Is this about a diet? Because you know diets don't work and we do not shame each other for food choices."

"Oh, no, I hate diets," Rachel said, forcing a little laugh.

"Then enjoy the cookie," Ms. Deats said. "Self-nourishment is very important. I don't want you to think that just because I'm upset with you about last night, I don't want you to enjoy yourself on your last day here."

"Eat the cookie, Rachel," Gertie said. "It's amazing! Where'd you get these?"

Ms. Deats, Sivan, and Gertie looked at her expectantly.

"Oh, it's a long story," Rachel said faintly, and popped the cookie in her mouth.

"Ooh, looks like they've got breakfast ready!" Ms. Deats said happily.

They ate and ate and ate. Sivan and Gertie chattered a bit, but Rachel was uncharacteristically quiet.

"You okay?" Sivan asked, concerned.

"Fine," Rachel said. "I'm just tired."

"All right, everyone!" Mr. Kenner said. "Time to get on the bus and head to the White House!"

The bus ride to the White House took about thirty or forty minutes with all the D.C. rush hour traffic, and by the time she stepped off the bus, Gertie felt really good. Really relaxed. It was amazing what a nice breakfast with good friends could do to lighten one's hangover. As they stood in line to meet their tour guide, she found herself smiling broadly at everyone—even Peighton, Kaylee, and Brooklynn, who shot her confused looks.

"Why is she looking at us?" Kaylee asked, loud enough for Gertie to hear.

Gertie's heart swelled with love for this girl who had been her enemy until the previous evening's détente.

"Because you're beautiful," Gertie said, and she meant it. She had never noticed how utterly angelic Kaylee's features were before. She looked like something out of one of those Renaissance paintings, except prettier.

"Doesn't Kaylee look like an angel, Rachel?" Gertie said, tapping her friend on the shoulder. "Rachel. Rachel. Rachel. Rachel. Rachel." She had to say "Rachel" a few more times before Rachel turned around.

"Isn't Kaylee beautiful?" Gertie said.

"Um, sure, yeah," Rachel said, her eyes darting around nervously. "Definitely." Then she turned back around and commenced staring at her feet.

"Weird," Kaylee whispered to Peighton and Brooklynn. "I always thought the one that looks like a boy was the only lesbian."

"Just because somebody thinks you're pretty doesn't make them gay," Peighton said. "She was just being nice."

Sivan watched this play out. Her eyes were heavy lidded, but she looked utterly fascinated.

"Cool," Sivan said, dragging out the syllable. "Cooooooool."

"You okay?" Peighton asked uncertainly.

"I know, right?" Sivan said, and started giggling. She didn't stop until Ms. Deats introduced their tour guide, and even then Sivan had to keep a hand clamped over her mouth for a few minutes straight.

Gertie raised her hand when the tour guide asked if anyone had any questions.

"I do!" she sang. "I dooooo!"

"Oh, fuck," Rachel muttered, still staring at her feet. "Oh, fuck. Oh, fuck. Oh, fuck."

"Yes?" the tour guide asked with a friendly smile.

"Are we going to meet the president?" Gertie asked excitedly.

Everyone laughed. The chaperones shushed them. Gertie just smiled broadly, happy that they were all happy too.

"That's actually our most common question," said the tour guide, a handsome young man named DeShawn. "But the answer is no, unfortunately, the president doesn't have enough time in his day to meet most people who come through the White House. Every once in a while we might catch a glimpse of him walking with his Secret Service team, but that's VERY rare. It has only happened on one tour I've ever led, and that was two years ago."

"Cooool," Sivan said, and let out a giggle.

"It's good to see such enthusiasm," DeShawn said. "Everyone's in a good mood today, huh?"

"Fuck," Rachel muttered softly.

"I'm sorry, what was that, miss?" DeShawn asked. "Did you have a question?"

"Nothing," Rachel said. "Sorry."

"You okay, Rachel?" Ms. Deats.

"Yes," Rachel said.

"Okay, good," Ms. Deats said. She gave Rachel a quizzical look, but Rachel was staring at the ground again.

DeShawn led them into the first room on the tour and began explaining the significance of a particular painting. It was lost on Gertie, Sivan, and Rachel. Gertie was busy appreciating the intricate beauty of the carpet on which they stood. Sivan was peering around at everyone's faces and giggling when they noticed her looking. Rachel was staring at her feet. Hard.

After a few rooms full of ornate decorations and, of course, lots of American history, Gertie realized something: she really had to pee. She crept over to Ms. Deats and smiled at her adoringly.

"Yes, Gertie?" Ms. Deats asked.

"You're so pretty," Gertie said.

"Oh, my!" Ms. Deats said, blushing. "Well, thank you, Gertie."

She paused, and Gertie smiled at her sweetly.

"Was there something else, Gertie?" Ms. Deats asked.

"I have to pee real bad," Gertie said.

"Well, we'll take a bathroom break when DeShawn says we can," Ms. Deats said. DeShawn overheard her.

"We're actually coming up on the public restroom right now," he said. "It's the perfect time for a bathroom break."

It turned out that nobody had to use the boys' room except for Carter Bump and Brock Chuddford, who was asking Carter tons of questions about everything De-Shawn was saying (by this point in the trip, Carter knew a little bit about how to translate things into Brock-speak, and he even found himself saying things he didn't usually say, like "bro" and "chill." Rachel found it adorable, but in a different way than she'd previously found Carter Bump adorable.) And nobody had to use the girls' room but Gertie, Sivan, and Rachel.

Gertie floated into the restroom. Sivan tripped, letting out a snort of laughter. And Rachel shuffled in and quickly took refuge in a stall.

"I feel so amazing," Gertie said as she peed. "Don't you girls feel amazing?"

"Totally," Sivan said, laughing. "This is the best trip ever. I heard they have a gender-netural restroom somewhere in the White House. Did you know that? Isn't that cool?"

"Um," Rachel said.

"What, Rach?" Gertie asked. She felt very warm inside, and really full but also kind of light at the same time? Like her skin was made of air? Like that. Whatever that felt like.

"That cookie," Rachel said.

"What about the cookie?" Gertie asked. "It was so good!"

"It had, um," Rachel started, and then she said something unintelligible.

"What?" Sivan asked.

"It had drugs in it," Rachel whispered. "They were hash cookies. I was going to tell you, but you grabbed them so fast and then Ms. Deats was there so I couldn't tell you the truth."

"*What?*" Gertie said, aghast. "What? Are you fucking kidding me?"

Sivan started laughing and laughing.

"What the FUCK!" Gertie's feel-good haze was gone, replaced with anger and swirling anxiety. She slammed her way out of the stall, and came face-to-face with the cuntriad.

"You guys did *drugs*?" Brooklynn said, a slow smile spreading across her face. "Like, at the White House?"

Rachel and Sivan came out of their stalls at the sound of her voice. Rachel looked terrified. Sivan stopped giggling and looked frightened.

"Did you buy drugs in the White House?" Kaylee asked, fascinated.

"No," Rachel said. "We would never do that. We're not on drugs. We're just, um . . . we are just tired."

"Sure you are," Peighton said, grinning at the girls. The cuntriad finished washing their hands and filed out of the bathroom.

"Oh, nooooo," Sivan said, grabbing her head. "Oh, noooo. Oh no oh no oh nooooo."

"We're gonna get expelled," Rachel said dully. "We are. This is it. This is the end."

"I can't believe you gave me a fucking drug cookie!" Gertie said. "I feel so fucking betrayed."

"It was an accident!" Rachel said. She looked almost ready to cry.

"Oh noooo," Sivan said. "Oh noooo. Oh nooo."

"Where did you even get hash cookies?" Gertie asked.

"I bought them off the preacher's kid who made us the fake IDs," Rachel said. "He dabbles in marijuana baking on the side. I was gonna *ask* if you wanted to get high, but then the cookies fell out and you just grabbed them and—I couldn't stop you!"

"Oh nooo," Sivan said. "Oh no." She was pacing back and forth. She definitely wasn't giggling anymore.

"And now we're high in the fucking White House!" Gertie said, feeling the panic crawl from her stomach to her throat. "I cannot believe you. This is the worst thing ever. We are not friends anymore!"

"Don't say that!" Rachel said, and she started to cry for real.

"True," Sivan said, pacing. "True. True. True."

"What are we gonna do?" Gertie asked hysterically.

They were all quiet for a moment. Then Sivan looked at them.

"We're gonna make a run for it," she said.

"If we run away, how will we eat?" Gertie asked tearfully.

"We'll hunt and gather," Sivan whispered to her own reflection in the mirror. "Like the Native Americans."

"We can hide somewhere in D.C. until we're not high anymore," Rachel said. "And then—and then we'll go home."

"How?" Gertie asked. "How will we go home?"

"I don't know," Rachel said. "We can hitchhike. Or ride bikes. Maybe we can rent bikes. We just—we need to get out of here." She was panicking too. They all were.

The restroom had two entrances, as it was located between two separate hallways. Rachel walked swiftly and with great purpose out the entrance that they had not used. The girls followed her and were immediately swept up in a group of reporters who were being herded into some room. Gertie and Sivan didn't know where Rachel was going, but *she* sure seemed to, so they followed her as she made a left down one hallway and a right down another, and then doubled back and went down yet another hallway, and suddenly there was a big glass door before them and Rachel pulled it open and they were suddenly in some kind of garden.

"Where the fuck are we?" Gertie cried. "All I see are rosebushes."

"Oh, God," Sivan said. "Oh God oh God oh God."

"Quick!" Rachel said. "Let's hide! Let's hide!" She dragged the girls behind a shrub, where they crouched, holding one another and shaking.

"This is the worst thing we've ever done in our whole lives," Gertie moaned. "This like a legit, real federal offense. Our parents are gonna kill us. Ms. Deats is gonna kill us. Mr. Kenner is definitely gonna kill us."

"I am so sorry," Rachel said, getting choked up again. "They're probably going to try us as adults. Oh God. I hate being sixteen. Where did our childhoods go?"

"It's okay," Gertie said, breaking down. "I love you girls."

"Love," Sivan said, tears running down her face. "Lots of love. Lots of love."

They all hugged and cried.

"Maybe we can stay out here for a while and just figure shit out," Rachel said. "We can just stay out here for like a few minutes or hours or days or something. We can build a shelter, and we can just live here. We can huddle together at night for warmth."

"It is a pretty nice place to live," came a male voice. "Though I prefer living in the White House itself, rather than the Rose Garden."

The girls looked up and squinted. The man's head moved to block the sun, and he peered curiously down at them. They recognized him immediately.

"Holy fucking shit," Rachel said. "Is that the mother-fucking president?"

"It is indeed," he said. "Now the question is, who are you and what are you doing in my Rose Garden?"

"Where are Gertie, Rachel, and Sivan?" Brian asked. "It's kind of been a while."

"They were in the bathroom," Alicia said. "Brooklynn, did you see them?"

"Yeah, but we just went to wash our hands and fix our hair," Brooklynn said.

"Did anything seem different? Did they seem sick?" Alicia asked.

Brooklynn opened her mouth, but Peighton cut in.

"They were fine," she said. "Totally normal. They're probably still in there."

"Okay," Alicia said, taking a deep breath. "Mr. Kenner, I'm going to the girls' room to find them."

"Of course," Brian said.

Alicia speed-walked to the bathroom and threw open the door.

There was no one inside.

"Oh, fuck," she said.

This was, to put it lightly, not fucking good.

She went back to Brian and whispered the news to him. Brian's face was ashen.

"Okay," he murmured. "Let's tell DeShawn."

"Oh, no," Alicia said, her heart beating fast, the nausea beginning to swirl. "What if this gets into the press? 'Flemington High School Students Lost in White House?'"

"Let's deal with one crisis at a time," Brian said soothingly. "We can handle this. We'll find them. This is the most heavily protected tourist destination in the United States. They probably just wandered off with another tour group. And hey, if after all this we still get fired—more time to catch up on *Doctor Who*."

Alicia looked at him. Was he really making a joke at a time like this?

He was.

She couldn't figure out if she wanted to hit him or kiss him.

Alicia rushed to tell DeShawn what was going on.

"We just lost them," Alicia said. "They went to the bathroom and then they just disappeared. I . . . I feel terrible."

"Ma'am," DeShawn said after she explained the situation. "I'm sure they just wandered off in the wrong direction by mistake. It does happen. But this is a security issue. I'm going to have to alert the Secret Service."

"I was afraid you were going to say that," Alicia said with a sigh.

"So you're the president," Rachel said with wonder. They were sitting in the Oval Office, the girls on an elegant sofa, the president in a chair that was probably worth like fifty thousand dollars.

"I am indeed," said the president.

"No shit," Gertie said, propping her chin up in her hand. "That is fucking crazy."

"I suppose it is, depending on your opinion of the campaign we ran," the president said with a smile. "Let me get you girls some water." He gestured to an aide, who disappeared into another room and reappeared within an instant with bottles of water.

"People are always getting us bottles of water," Rachel said to Gertie. "Like last night, with Octavia Thunderpussy."

"I know, right?" Gertie said. "It's really nice."

Sivan said nothing. She was staring very intently at the president.

"So, I'm the president," he said. "We've established that. And you all are—"

"Should we tell him our names?" Gertie whispered loudly to Sivan and Rachel. Sivan shrugged. Rachel appeared to mull it over.

"I can find out pretty easily," the president said. "You know that, right?"

"That's a solid point," Sivan said, nodding. "Yeah. We should tell him who we are."

"I'm Gertie," said Gertie.

"I'm Rachel," said Rachel.

"I'm Sivan," said Sivan. "And I have some thoughts I'd like to share with you on the Israeli-Palestinian conflict."

"You and everybody else who comes through this office," the president said.

"Yes, but mine are correct," Sivan said.

"Fair enough," said the president. "Go right ahead."

While Sivan expounded on her theory of an integrated one-state solution, Rachel and Gertie drank their water and smiled. Then Rachel noticed something on the wall and gasped.

"Is that JF *fucking* K?" she demanded, pointing at a portrait.

"Well, we don't call him that exactly," the president said, smiling. "But yes, that's President Kennedy. A real American hero."

"Didn't he totally have sex with Marilyn Monroe, like, in the White House?" Rachel asked.

"I'm not sure about that," the president said. "I think it's fair to say he had some adventures in his day. I think that much is a matter of public record." He cleared his throat. "So, what brings you young women to the capital?"

"Well, this is our school trip," Gertie said.

"Wonderful!" the president said. "You know, a lot of American high schools go on their senior class trip to Washington, D.C. And education is one of my biggest priorities, especially the education of women and girls. You going to college later this year?"

"Georgetown," all three girls said in unison. They looked at each other and tried not to giggle. Sivan slapped a hand over her mouth again and snorted into it.

"Great!" the president said. "You must get excellent grades. If you already know where you're going, you must've applied Early Decision."

"I do get excellent grades," Sivan said. "I really do. It's not a lie."

"I wouldn't think it would be," the president said. He looked at the girls carefully.

"You know, college is a time to make good choices," he said casually. "Safe choices. Healthy choices. Sometimes we do things as teenagers that are silly or foolish, because we're pushing our boundaries."

"Oh my God, Gertie, he sounds like your parents!" Rachel said excitedly.

"Mine too," Sivan said.

"You must have great parents," the president said. "And

very practical ones too. They know, like I do, that we all make mistakes. Sometimes these mistakes are rather serious, and we're lucky to get a second chance. Since I've made mistakes in my own life, I understand what it's like to, say, goof off a bit on a school trip."

"Is he talking about us?" Gertie whispered to Rachel.

"I think so," Rachel said.

"Is he mad?" Gertie asked.

"I'm not mad," the president said. "Also, I can hear everything you're saying. I am literally four feet away from you and you're whispering really, really loudly."

Gertie turned bright red.

"What I'm saying is, if you girls got up to some shenanigans today, maybe on a dare or what have you, that's all right," the president said. "I assume it's how you ended up in my Rose Garden. But you need to recognize that not everybody in life is going to be as understanding as I'm being right now. For example, my Secret Service team was ready to drag you off for some pretty serious questioning."

"No way!" Gertie said fearfully. "Your Secret Service guys saw us?"

"They've been tracking you since you entered this building," the president said. "Not my personal team, but another team that manages security for the whole White House. They track everybody. Especially people who end up in places where they're not supposed to be. You know there are cameras everywhere in this building, right? We're being watched right now."

"Surveillance," Sivan said. "The state is everywhere. We live in a Panopticon."

"I appreciate the Foucault reference, Sivan," the president said. "But actually, you don't live here, specifically. I actually do live here, specifically. And so does my family. And when intruders go into restricted areas—even nice young women like yourselves—the Secret Service notices and reacts immediately. In this case, I happened to be saying hi to the building surveillance team, and when they wanted to send in a team to extract you, I said, 'Look. I have teenage daughters. Let me talk to them first.'"

"No way," Rachel said in wonder. "You did that for us?"

"Well, yes," the president said. "I had to fight them on it too. They thought you could be armed. But I had a hunch that was not the case."

"Oh, no," Sivan said. "We're pacifists."

"Although we're big military supporters," Rachel said.

"Well, I have some issues with the military industrial complex," Sivan said.

"We're very patriotic," Rachel said.

"I take issue with patriotism that looks like nationalism, though," Sivan said.

"How are you even friends?" the president asked.

"Nursery school," the two girls said in unison. Gertie was busy gazing at the president's suit. It was really a nice suit. Like it was probably the nicest suit she'd ever seen in her whole life.

"Oh, that's very nice," the president said. "Anyway, are you girls picking up what I'm saying?"

"You know, don't you?" Gertie asked, very matter-of-factly.

"Gertie!" Rachel said. "He has no idea!"

"Yeah, we're cool," Sivan said. "He's cool. Everything's cool."

The president sighed and shook his head.

"Gertie," he said. "If there's one thing a life in politics has taught me, it's that I don't KNOW something until somebody tells me. And some things—some things I'd just rather not know. You know?"

Comprehension dawned on Gertie.

"Ohhhh," she said slowly, nodding. "Oh, I see. Okay. Yes."

The president looked at the girls conspiratorially.

"Besides," he said, lowering his voice. "I was eighteen too, once."

"Oh, we're not—" Gertie started to say, and Rachel slapped a hand over her mouth.

"We're not ever going to do anything like this ever again," Rachel said. "And we really appreciate your patience and understanding, sir. Thank you."

"Yeah, thank you," Sivan said.

"Thank you so fucking much," Gertie said through Rachel's hand.

"Ew, Gertie," Rachel said. "You kind of got spit on my hand."

"Sorry," Gertie said.

"Now, let's get you back to your group," the president said.

"Well, it was nice meeting you, sir," Rachel said, and the girls got up to leave.

"Oh, I'm coming with you," the president said. "Probably make your teachers less mad at you."

"Oh, shit," Sivan said. "Are they mad at us?"

"My guess is that they are worried sick," the president said. "But we're going to make it better, all right?"

"Okay," Sivan said. "Our teachers are Ms. Deats and Mr. Kenner, by the way. They might be kind of in love, we're not sure."

"That's very sweet, Sivan," the president said, rising to his feet. As if on cue, three Secret Service agents entered the room.

"They're going to escort us out," the president said as the girls stared in wide-eyed wonder.

"They're really cute," Rachel said to no one in particular.

"Yes, that's why I picked them," the president said. "Come along now, girls."

Ms. Deats's heart was in her throat. The entire group was lined up against one wall of a hallway, waiting quietly as Alicia and Brian paced back and forth. Even Peighton, Brooklynn, and Kaylee looked uncharacteristically somber, perhaps because Alicia looked so openly worried. No one was used to seeing sweet, hippie-dippie Ms. Deats in such a state.

"I'm sure they're fine," DeShawn said. "Really, ma'am. Sir. I wouldn't worry too much."

"It's been too long," Alicia said.

"DeShawn is right, Alicia," Brian said. He was pale, but he was keeping it together. "They're fine. This is the safest place in the world for them to get lost."

"I failed them," Alicia said, shaking her head. "This is my fault. I should've escorted them to the bathroom instead of supervising out here."

"Yo, Ms. Deats," Brock Chuddford said. "If I may? You're a great teacher. You didn't do anything wrong. Sometimes shit just happens. Chicks go off and do weird shit because of hormones or whatever. You can't control that."

"Thank you, Brock," Brian said. "That was very . . . encouraging."

"Yes, Brock, thank you," Alicia said faintly.

Brock Chuddford looked at Carter Bump.

"I said shit, though," he said apologetically. "That's inappropriate, right, bro?"

"That's okay, man," Carter Bump said. "I mean, bro."

Brock smiled and gave Carter Bump a good-natured noogie, just like he did to all his favorite friends. Brock's other friends sighed audibly. Apparently they were just going to have to accept this weird little kid into their brotherhood.

And then a chatter of excitement ran through the hallway like lightning. There was another tour group down the hall, and they exploded in gasps and claps and cheers. Alicia and Brian craned their necks to see what was going on, and that's when the crowd parted and they saw the president of the United States of America.

And Gertie.

And Sivan.

And Rachel.

And a team of really stern-looking Secret Service guys.

"No fucking way," Alicia said, her eyes wide. Then she realized what she'd said.

"Oh, students," she said. "I am so sorry."

"No way, Ms. Deats," Brock Chuddford said. "That was cool as hell. Now I feel less bad about saying 'shit.'"

"Everybody stand up straight," Brian said quickly. "And be very, very polite. The president is coming this way."

Brooklynn, Peighton, and Kaylee looked at one another in disbelief.

"What in the fuck?" Brooklynn screeched.

"Brooklynn, please!" Brian said. "Shh!"

When the president reached them, he was all smiles.

"Mr. Kenner?" he said, and shook Brian's hand. "And you must be Ms. Deats," he said, shaking Alicia's hand.

The two of them were shocked beyond belief. Brian got it together enough to say, "It is an honor to meet you, sir," but Alicia just stared.

"I believe I have something you're looking for," he said.

Alicia looked at the girls and shook her head.

"I have no idea what to say," she said finally. "Except that I am so sorry our girls got lost. And we will deal with them in an appropriate manner, Mr. President."

Gertie, Sivan, and Rachel cringed.

"Got lost?" the president said. "I think you're mistaken, Ms. Deats. I had them brought to my office so that I could talk to them about matters of great national importance."

"You—you did?" Alicia asked, utterly confused.

"Absolutely," the president said. "It's something I like to do with visitors to the White House every once in a while, especially young ones. Hear what the young people are interested in. Keep current on their issues. They are our future, after all." He smiled at Gertie, Sivan, and Rachel, who looked at him as if he were their savior (which, in fact, he kind of was).

"So . . . they didn't get lost . . . or wander off," Brian said. "You wanted to talk to them."

"Yes, sir," the president said. "And I'm so glad I did. We spoke about education and they expressed deep admiration for the both of you and all of the work that you do."

"They—they did?" Brian asked.

"Really?" Alicia said.

"Indeed they did," the president said. "Couldn't say enough good things about you. Honestly, it made me feel pretty good about the state of education in this country, to hear three intelligent young people praise their teachers like that."

"I cannot believe this is happening," Brooklynn hissed to Peighton, who was smiling a little.

"Just go with it, B," Peighton murmured.

"Well, I have to get going," the president said. "Would you like to take a picture?"

"I—I—yes, I have my cell phone," Alicia said. "Yes."

"I'll take it for you," DeShawn said. He looked shyly at the president, who patted him on the back.

And that's how Gertie, Sivan, Rachel, Alicia Deats, Brian Kenner, and the president of the United States ended up posing for a photo along with the entire sophomore class of Flemington High School. No one in the photo was grinning more widely than Alicia Deats and Brian Kenner. And no one was frowning harder than Brooklynn. She was the only one frowning, in fact. Everybody else was feeling pretty giddy.

"You two make a pretty great team," the president told Alicia and Brian before he left. He had a mischievous twinkle in his eye.

"Oh, well, thank you, sir," Alicia said.

"Were you . . . assigned to do this trip together?"

"Um," Brian said. "Well. I had signed up to do it, and then Alicia here—I mean Ms. Deats—she volunteered to come along, and I thought it was a great idea because the students trust her and love her so much. I'm more of a by-the-numbers guy, but she—she's got a lot of heart. And I need that. I mean, the kids need that. I need the kids to have that. Is what I mean."

"Oh my *God*," Brooklynn whispered to Kaylee and Peighton. "He's like totally in love with her. Fucking gross."

"B," Peighton whispered back. "I love you? I really do? But you need to shut the fuck up, because love is beautiful."

Brooklynn looked stung.

The president bid his farewell. But before he walked away, he paused and asked, "So, what's the name of your school, Alicia and Brian? I didn't actually ever get that."

"Flemington High School," Alicia said proudly.

The president smiled.

"Flemington High School," he said. "That's not a name I'll soon forget."

"Sir, you're needed in the Oval Office," a Secret Service agent said. "Russia is on the line."

The Secret Service team hustled the president away, but not before he shot Gertie, Sivan, and Rachel a pointed look. They smiled back at him with evident gratitude.

"Thank you," Gertie mouthed, and then he was gone.

Alicia looked at Brian. Brian looked at Alicia.

Brian opened his arms wide.

"Bring it in," he said. "Everybody. Big Flemington family hug."

"But be respectful of your neighbor's personal space," Alicia said quickly.

"Naturally," Brian said. "But seriously, guys. Bring it in."

And they all did.

The bus ride home can best be described in two words: "exhausted" and "jubilant." It was a heady combination.

Rachel, Gertie, and Sivan were the stars of the show. They recounted a *highly* edited version of the story to their teachers and classmates, all of whom were very impressed.

"I even got to talk to him about my suggestions for peace in the Middle East," Sivan said.

"Good for you, Sivan," Alicia Deats said, nodding her head vigorously. "You used your moment wisely."

"Now everybody gets a treat," Brian announced. He and Alicia grinned at each other.

"You get your cell phones back!" they exclaimed together, and a roar of joy rose up from the group.

"I'm going to post the photo with the president on my Instagram, so everybody can grab it from there," Alicia said. "And I'm emailing it to all your parents too!"

They all knew Ms. Deats' Instagram because it was just a bunch of inspirational quotes of the day that she made them read every single day. This was the first time any of them had actually been excited to go to her Instagram.

They handed out the student's cell phones, and soon the bus was abuzz with phone calls and texts to and from delighted parents.

Alicia Deats's phone rang with an incoming number that she recognized as the school office. She picked it up eagerly.

"Yes?" she asked.

"Alicia Fucking Deats, YOU are my teacher of the year," the principal's voice boomed through the line.

"No way!" Alicia said.

"Well, not really," the principal said. "I mean, that's voted on by the entire faculty at the end of the year, and it'll probably go to Patti Bump like it does every year. But just right now? In this moment? YOU are my teacher of the year. That photo is going to get us such amazing press."

"Well, Brian Kenner had something to do with it too," Alicia said. He smiled at her and surreptitiously squeezed her arm. She fought the urge to jump on him right then and there.

"I'm sure he did," the principal said. "I am so proud of both of you. You're a great team."

"That's what the president said!" Alicia exclaimed.

"Well, he's a smart man," the principal said. "I didn't vote for him, but he's smart."

The bus ride seemed to fly by. Once they hit New Jersey, Alicia had the bus driver turn on an oldies station, and all the students sang along to "Respect" by Aretha Franklin and "Build Me Up Buttercup" by the Foundations and a bunch of other songs they were used to hearing at their grandparents' houses.

They sang all the rest of the way home.

When the bus pulled into the school parking lot, they saw to their surprise that all the parents were gathered on the front lawn of the school. The parents started cheering as soon as they saw the bus, and the students pressed their faces against the windows.

"Wow," Brock Chuddford said. "I've never seen my mom look so happy to see me. Usually she just looks stressed."

"My mom looks really happy too," Carter Bump marveled. "Hey look, they're talking to each other."

"That's good," Brock said. "My dad says my mom needs more friends, to get her off his ass."

When they got off the bus, they were all immediately enfolded in parental hugs. Gertie, Sivan, and Rachel had inexplicable headaches, but other than that they felt really great.

The Finkelsteins were chatting with Gertie's parents when Sivan felt a tap on her shoulder. She turned around, and there was Peighton. Instinctively, Sivan stepped back.

"It's okay," Peighton said. "I'm not here to be mean to you. For once."

"I know," Sivan said. "After last night, I know. But, um . . . what are you here for?"

Peighton blushed.

"To say I'm sorry," Peighton said shyly. "I know me and my friends treat you and your friends like shit. And it's not like I expect you to want to be best buddies now or something, but I just want you to know that I know I've been wrong in the way I've treated you. Mostly it's because I'm jealous of how—open you are. I wish I could be that way too."

Sivan was speechless.

"I think, sometimes, there are things about you that . . . that remind me of myself," Peighton said, shifting her weight from one leg to the other and bouncing her foot nervously. "You know what I mean?" She looked down at the ground, then right into Sivan's eyes.

"Yeah," Sivan said. "I do. You can always call me or text me or whatever if you want to talk."

"I might do that," Peighton said. Then she walked back

to her own parents, who were standing with Kaylee's parents and Brooklynn's parents.

Rachel stood a little away from everyone else. Now her parents were talking to Carter Bump's mother, who was nodding politely even though she was probably getting an earful of church talk. Carter joined Rachel.

"So, um," Rachel said. "About last night . . ."

"We can forget about last night if you want, Rachel," Carter said. "We were both drunk and we said some things . . ."

"They were true things, though," Rachel said. "Weren't they?"

"Well, yeah," Carter said. "I mean, I think they were. I was being honest. I really think you're into me."

"And I really think you're into me," Rachel said.

"Maybe we're both right," Carter said.

"So what do we do?" Rachel asked.

"Well, what would you usually do in this situation?" Carter said.

"Fuck you behind the gym," Rachel said automatically.

"Okay, we're going to do the opposite of that," Carter said.

"Fuck . . . in the art studio?" Rachel said uncertainly.

"No," Carter said. "Not at first, anyway. We're going to get to know each other. I'm going to take you on a date."

"A date?" Rachel was shocked. "Like, a real date? With flowers and everything?"

"With flowers and everything," Carter Bump said. "And no sex for a while."

"Wow," Rachel said.

"You in?" Carter said.

"Yeah," Rachel said. "I'm in. But what will we do if we don't have sex?"

"We'll talk, Rachel," Carter said.

"Wow," Rachel said. "You're blowing my mind."

"I have that effect on women," Carter said.

Gertie watched with wonder as Peighton and Sivan had what appeared to be a perfectly civilized conversation, and Carter Bump and Rachel had—wait, what the hell kind of conversation was Rachel having with Carter Bump? They were smiling at each other like total dorks.

Holy shit, did Rachel and Carter Bump *like* each other?

Gertie marveled at what madness life could bring.

Then she felt a tap on her shoulder.

She turned around, and there was Danny Bryan. He smiled down at her and she struggled to stay on her feet.

"What?" she asked of no one in particular. "What?"

"Hi," he said.

"How are you here?" she asked, confused.

"We got back to Lindbergh early and I figured you'd be getting to FHS around now," Danny said. "Looks like I was right."

"You came here just to see me?" Gertie asked in disbelief.

"I came here just to see you," Danny said. "Oh, where are your mom and dad?"

"They're here somewhere," Gertie said. "Over behind that tree, talking to some parents. Why?"

"Cool, they're not looking," Danny said, and he pulled her to him.

"I didn't get to do this last night," he whispered in her ear. "And I didn't want to wait another seven years."

And then he kissed her—like a real kiss, like lips meeting lips, and lips parting and tongue meeting tongue and it was not at all gross as Gertie had suspected her first kiss might be, but was in fact perfect and amazing and even better than masturbating about Danny Bryan had ever been. He pressed her to him and she wasn't positive but she thought she felt something hard, and made a mental note to ask Rachel about that.

When they parted, she stared up at him, her eyes wide.

"Here?" she said. "I mean—you came here, for this?"

"For you," he said. "I'd go anywhere for you."

And if there was any doubt whether she grabbed him and kissed him again then, even with all the parents and students milling around, right there in broad daylight, in front of everybody, on the front lawn of Flemington High School while cars whizzed past on Route 31 . . .

. . . well, of course she fucking did.

FROM: Alicia Deats
TO: Karen Fox
SUBJECT: You survived!

Karen, I cannot tell you how proud I am of you. Don't you dare feel bad about that emergency phone call from the bathroom at the National Portrait Gallery. A student sticking gum on a portrait of George Washington would be enough to give anybody a panic attack. I'm glad you kept those Xanax I gave you. And that they didn't call the D.C. police.

I will admit I'm flattered you used some of my tactics, and impressed you thought to tape all the doors with *duct* tape every single night. Yes, duct tape takes the paint off the walls and you will have to pay out of your own pocket, but hey! Rookie mistake!

Things were quiet on the home front except for one thing, and you must swear up and down you won't tell anybody—I'm pregnant. Yes, Brian Kenner finally put a baby inside me. You know I was big on a child-free life-style for the first few years of our marriage, but we've ac-tually been trying for a year because we decided we were ready. I've been taking this weird herbal fertility mix that I get from the herbalist who works out of the yoga studio. I guess it worked, or maybe doing it like mad with no condom or birth control just eventually leads to this sort of thing.

At any rate, next school year they're going to need someone to teach AP History while I'm on maternity leave, and I figure you're as good a choice as any, Ms. Fox. When the time is right, I'll put in a good word with the principal. I know you'll only be a second-year teacher, but fuck it. You're my favorite and I've taught you all my secret tricks, anyway, Young Padawan Learner. (That's a Star Wars joke, if you didn't know. Sometimes I forget that not everybody talks to each other the way Brian and I do. He wants to call the kid Anakin, and I'm like, "Um, no, that does not bode well for anyone." So it's up for debate.)

So be good, little Karen. Take good care of yourself. I'll see you soon. I'm proud of you.

Love,
Alicia

P.S. Do you want a fuckload of weed? Because I have a lot and I can't do anything with it for nine months. Kids ruin everything.

ACKNOWLEDGMENTS

This book would not exist if Marshall Lewy hadn't mysteriously shown up at a panel I was on at the Silver Lake Public Library in 2014, so I thank him for finding a justifiable reason to cut out of work early and go author scouting. Thanks also to Cecil Castellucci for putting me on said panel!

Jordan Hamessley has been a delightful editor and I appreciate that she made me put in a dirtier sex scene for Alicia and Brian. That's the kind of editorial advice you want.

Thanks to the entire team at Adaptive Books and Adaptive Studios; Jane Fransson for being there early on to guide this ship; Deb Shapiro for PR wizardry; Diana Kolsky for the brilliant cover; the dead trees that made the pages of the printed galleys and books. I love you forever, dead trees. I will plant new baby trees in your honor. Thank you to Emily Epstein White for copyediting the living FUCK out of the manuscript and for being my friend for many years. I remember the first time I walked into a comedy club in the back of a bubble tea shop in Chinatown and there you were. "Maybe she'll be my friend," I thought. KABOOM! HERE WE ARE! Thanks also goes to copyediting magician Laaren Brown!

Thank you to John DeVore, who motivated me, encouraged me, celebrated with me, hugged me when I needed it, and reminded me that our beautiful Shih-Tzu/Chihuahua/toy poodle/greyhound mix, Morley Safer, still needed playtime even if I was busy struggling with how to write the dirty sex scene demanded by one Jordan Hamessley. In the time it took me to write this book, John did many amazing things, including winning two James Beard Awards for an essay about Taco Bell. He is one cool cat.

Thank you to my family, the Benincasas and the Donnellys and all our extended families (Kozielecs, other Benincasas, Stahlins, Persicos, Hodnetts, Faersteins, Francises, etc.) for being so unbelievably supportive and enthusiastic. A special *mazel tov* to my brother, Steve, and my future sister-in-law, Elaine.

Just a few of the people who inspired me during this writing process: the brilliant Jill Soloway, who makes art that saves lives and also makes me laugh my ass off; the hilarious Michael Ian Black, who is pretty much a comic genius in my book and is very handsome and debonair to boot; the incredibly gifted Lena Dunham, who ought to be known as much for her generosity of spirit as she is for her wit and talent and butt; the incomparable Diablo Cody, with whom I have been honored to work for the past few years; Rebecca Trent, who gave me an excellent TARDIS blanket; and Roxane Gay, who kicks all kinds of ass. Thank you Tom Perrotta for everything. You rock my face off. Thanks also to Albert Berger and Ron Yerxa for believing in Gertie and Alicia.

Thanks to my literary agent, Scott Mendel, who deserves to be the subject of laudatory ballads written by wandering Renaissance-era performers and is what the kids call "a true mensch." Thanks to the excellent Doug Johnson, Melissa Orton and Josh Pearl at ICM and the scamp known as Sean Lawton at Keppler Speakers. (HI DARLENE!)

A final thanks to the britches and witches of SHOUTY-CAMP. You know who you are.

Sara Benincasa is an award-winning comedian and author of *Real Artists Have Day Jobs, Great* and *Agorafabulous!: Dispatches from My Bedroom*, a book based on her critically acclaimed solo show about panic attacks and agoraphobia. Her comedy has won praise from the *Chicago Tribune, CNN, The Guardian,* and *The New York Times.*

ALSO AVAILABLE FROM ADAPTIVE BOOKS

Slim, successful, and soon to marry the man of her dreams, Katie Cravens is leading the life she always wanted. As the face and CEO of Pasta Pronto, a "Carbs for the Calorie-Conscious" line of frozen food, Katie chooses to live life like one of her Slimline Spaghetti dinners —no mess, no surprises, and everything tied up in a neat little package. But when Katie's fiancé runs off with another woman and a quality control fiasco sends her customers running for the hills, it's time for Katie to make a change.

Her company's salvation presents itself in the form of a partnership opportunity with the legendary Ristorante Caramelli of Rome, and Katie has no other choice but to jet off to Italy to convince gorgeous, hotheaded co-owner Luca Caramelli that she's a worthy partner. Gaining Luca's respect proves harder than Katie could have ever imagined, however, when he insists that she must learn how to cook—and how to eat—true Italian food before he will ever agree to their companies' partnership.

Katie and Luca's tension in Italy mounts into a fierce public rivalry that finally erupts back in the States with a nationally televised cooking competition. As Katie tries to channel her inner Mario Batali to win the competition, she must choose between the flavorless prepackaged life that she worked so hard to maintain and the mouthwatering uncertainty of a life chock full of carbohydrates and Caramellis.

LEARN MORE AT WWW.ADAPTIVESTUDIOS.COM